A SHOCKING REVELATION

"I wonder at *our* relationship," Mary said mildly, returning to her chair and arranging the shawl more satisfactorily about her shoulders. "I am, in case you
failed to note, a female. I should think that would put
me quite out of favor in your eyes."

"But you're not my demmed sister, or my mother.
And I must not be the slightest bit proper with you, as
I have just proven by the language I have chosen to use
in your presence. *That* makes all the difference, I assure you."

"So you think of me as, let us say, being one of the
'fellows'?" she asked, a trifle archly, frowning just a
little bit.

He raised the snifter to his lips, slumping even further into the chair's recesses. "Oh, hardly that, Mary.
I've never wondered what it would be like to lay down
with Mr. Bretwyn, or any of the other 'fellows', but I
assure you I have wondered the same about you . . ."

DISCOVER THE MAGIC OF REGENCY ROMANCES

ROMANTIC MASQUERADE   (3221, $3.95)
by Lois Stewart

Sabrina Latimer had come to London incognito on a fortune hunt. Disguised as a Hungarian countess, the young widow had to secure the ten thousand pounds her brother needed to pay a gambling debt. His debtor was the notorious ladies' man, Lord Jareth Tremayne. Her scheme would work if she did not fall prey to the charms of the devilish aristocrat. For Jareth was an expert at gambling and always played to win everything—and *everyone*—he could.

RETURN TO CHEYNE SPA   (3247, $2.95)
by Daisy Vivian

Very poor but ever-virtuous Elinor Hardy had to become a dealer in a London gambling house to be able to pay her rent. Her future looked dismal until Lady Augusta invited her to be her guest at the exclusive resort, Cheyne Spa. The one condition: Elinor must woo the unsuitable rogue who was in pursuit of the Duchess's pampered niece.

The unsuitable young man was enraptured with Elinor, but *she* had been struck by the devilishly handsome Tyger Dobyn. Elinor knew that Tyger was hardly the respectable, marrying kind, but unfortunately her heart did not agree!

A CRUEL DECEPTION   (3246, $3.95)
by Cathryn Huntington Chadwick

Lady Margaret Willoughby had resisted marriage for years, knowing that no man could replace her departed childhood love. But the time had come to produce an heir to the vast Willoughby holdings. First she would get her business affairs in order with the help of the new steward, the disturbingly attractive and infuriatingly capable Mr. Frank Watson; *then* she would begin the search for a man she could tolerate. If only she could find a mate with a *fraction* of the scandalously handsome Mr. Watson's appeal. . . .

The Marriage Mart
Teresa DesJardien

ZEBRA BOOKS
KENSINGTON PUBLISHING CORP.

To John—
my own personal Godfrey

ZEBRA BOOKS

are published by

Kensington Publishing Corp.
475 Park Avenue South
New York, NY 10016

First printing: February, 1992

Printed in the United States of America

Chapter One

Someone gasped in astonishment near Mary's ear, and that someone was her chaperone, whom Mary had thought to be well and away past the age of gasping. The experience was so novel that she turned at once to see what could have caused dear Mrs. Pennett to quite forget herself.

She saw a tall fellow who was no less than absolutely striking. The first thing one noted was that his hair was the most incredible color. She could only think to describe the color to herself as dark auburn, yet golden. The light caught upon the unusual color, making it appear almost as though he had a halo of golden light about those rich curls, and it was only after blinking several times that she convinced herself the nimbus had been imagined. But perhaps the inclination to view a celestial picture could be excused, for the gentleman in question was absolutely beautiful. His face was more refined than that of any statue she had ever seen, the features even and balanced. His nose was straight, his eyes, shaded as they were by auburn lashes, were the palest blue, perhaps the shade of the sky just before one ascended to the heavens. His mouth was perfect, so much so that she stared straight at his lips, as though searching for some flaw in that

5

lovely face. Finally she found one, when her eyes met his for the merest second as he swept his gaze over the crowd. For in his eyes was a light quite at contrast with the enchantment of his features. It was no angel that looked out upon the world from those orbs. Nay, it was an imp, a rascal, a rogue and perhaps, too, a little bit of a demon residing inside that exquisite frame.

Once she had seen the truth for herself, it was unmistakable in just the way he moved. He had a feline kind of grace; she knew instinctively that he was as capable of scampering to a safe distance as he was of instant combat. His was the nature that always looked for the advantage, and took it. The languid lift of his hand fooled her not at all, for the panther could stretch and yawn like the mildest house cat, but his strike would be deadly. He might seem relaxed and unprepared, but he was never any of that.

"What is his name?" Mary asked Mrs. Pennett, awe in her voice. There was no denying that her chaperone had recognized him.

" 'Tis The Blade," Mrs. Pennett said simply, as though she had explained all by the simple phrase. And indeed she had, for everyone had heard tell of "The Blade". He was none other than the Duke of Rothayne. Some said he had acquired the nickname 'Blade' for his rapier-quick wit, and others claimed it was for the wide swath he cut through the ladies.

"The Blade?" Mary said with some relish. "I thought he was banished from the Kingdom!"

"Apparently not," Mrs. Pennett said tersely as they both watched as the beautiful gentleman made his bow to their Regent. They watched as a pleasant—if not overly friendly—interchange took place, and continued to watch until their Prince made his farewells to Lady Jasper, his hostess. It could not have been made more clear that the royal person had stayed just long enough for the purpose of greeting the formerly out of favor Duke.

"I can scarce credit that the Prince would receive him," Mrs. Pennett said with scorn, a sound that was infrequent on her lips and therefore would have firmly caught Mary's attention if her gasp of recognition had not already done so.

"You know something!" Mary cried with relish. "Something scandalous. Tell me what it is."

Mrs. Pennett sniffed, and rocked her shoulders just a little, and demurred, "Oh, you know the tattle: he insulted the Prince and was forced to leave the country."

"Old news. No, you must tell me what it is that makes you bridle now, ages past that event."

"I shan't," Mrs. Pennett replied, coloring in a tell-tale fashion. When Mary merely gave her a steady, waiting look, she added quickly, "All I'll say is that it was just last week, and involved a married lady, a cemetery, and an indecency."

Mary's eyebrows rose, but an amused smile flitted into being. "I believe that is all I shall have from you on the matter, for, knowing none of the details, it is quite plain it would shock my delicate ears to hear it repeated," she said, her voice and manner indicating that she considered her own ears anything but delicate.

"It would!"

Mary turned back to watch the handsome gent, already surrounded by a bevy of the curious.

"But whatever The Blade was up to recently, it apparently was acceptable to Prinny. This Rothayne cannot be so wicked as you would have it," Mary said to herself, earning a hard look from her chaperone. She gave a puckish grin in return, and said, "Tut, tut, Gladys. You need not fear. I shall not make a cake of

7

myself over the fellow." She smiled a somewhat self-mocking smile, one that left her chaperone frowning disapprovingly.

"I despair of you," said Mrs. Pennett.

"You are not the first to do so."

Mary was the thorn in her family's collective side, for at the advanced age of 28 she had never married. She was not a beauty, but she was well enough in appearance. She often claimed there was nothing wrong with a single one of her features — she had just had the misfortune to have those upon her face which did not belong together. Her mother chided her for such words, her father 'hmmphed' and frowned, and her older sister and younger brother paid not the least attention at all, having heard much the same for twenty-odd years.

To compensate for her 'average but fine looks' her mother made sure her daughter was dressed in the finest, newest gowns; the combs and ribbons and pearls in her light chestnut hair were of quality, and she strove mightily to see that Mary's carriage and social skills were the most refined to be found in any sitting room. Of the latter the poor woman sometimes despaired of late, for it was quite obvious her daughter had decided she was upon the shelf, and that the restrictions to her tongue and manners ought no longer be so restraining anymore. So Mary had much her own way these days, although it must be said to her mother's credit that (despite a large and noisy temper tantrum at the age of 25) Mary had not persuaded her mother to do away with the use of a chaperone.

Now, at 28, she was resigned to the company of her custodian, and indeed took real pleasure in the older woman's company. Mrs. Pennett had been married for a brief five years, and had lost her husband to the sea. To her misfortune, there had been no pension, no income at all left to her, and no children, so she had found work as a nanny. It had proved to be a happy day when she had first met a bright-eyed, mildly belligerent, five-year-old Mary, and now it was hard to imagine the household without her. Mary had been known to tease her companion a little, saying she could *never* marry, for what would become of Mrs. Pennett? To which that lady had promptly replied, "Go ahead and wed then, Miss Mary, for I'd be even more useful these days in the nursery." Mary had just laughed, never letting on to her family that there was a real and true pang in her chest whenever she thought about the fact that she seemed destined to live her life without children of her own to love.

In fact, it was that very pang that had persuaded her to attend yet another cotillion. For although she had given up all hopes of attracting the handsome young men who attended these marriage marts, she had finally decided it might be acceptable to find an older gentleman with whom to settle down. Oh yes, her starry-eyed dreams of love and romance would have to be put aside, but those dreams were changing anyway into something a little more mature. Now, what she dreamed of most was a household of her own to run exactly as she pleased, filled to capacity with laughing, running, "Mummy-I-need-a-hug"-crying children. For that, she could give up manly affection. For that, she could bear to live with someone to whom she was less than fully attracted.

Her family was not wealthy, but most comfortably settled. She would bring a dowry to a marriage, but it was not of a size to attract fortune hunters, and for that she could only be grateful. If she had been unable to find someone to love, at least she had not been pestered by those who were pretending to do so for the sake of an income. She was the strangest of all social

9

creatures: not pretty, not ugly, not poor, not wealthy. She had a sparkling wit and a learned mind, but those things were worthless on the march toward matrimony. Or at least, so it seemed to young men.

Now, the *older* men, she had come to realize, might actually have some appreciation of her gifts. If a man was looking for a competent hostess, or a dinner and theatre companion, or someone to read to him if his eyes were bad, or to help him get about while leaning on her arm . . . why, she certainly qualified in all those areas.

"What are you thinking about, Puss? You've the strangest look on your face," Mrs. Pennett interrupted her thoughts.

Mary smiled, again at herself, and answered, "I was thinking that I must not attach myself to a man who is too ancient, for his main purpose will be to beget offspring. We must find one that is capable of the task."

"Mary!" Mrs. Pennett cried, utterly shocked by the words, if not the intent. She was the only soul in the world that had heard the recent and resigned truth from Miss Mary's lips, that she had finally made up her mind to wed. Mrs. Pennett alone had been allowed a glimpse of the anguish that flashed in those brown eyes when they passed baby-filled arms on the street. She alone knew that a youthful dream had come crashing down, surrounded by the sound of a loudly ticking clock that grew ever louder as each birthday passed. And when Mary tossed back her head and declared how she enjoyed being a maiden aunt, it was only Mrs. Pennett that knew how thoroughly the lady was lying.

So it was that Mrs. Pennett knew a little more of her charge's mind than the other way around. Mary had perhaps an inkling, but nowhere near the whole of it, of just how much Mrs. Pennett was resolved to see that a wedding *did* come forth from among these aged fellows—and the sooner, the better.

"Perhaps you should ask about and see which of the 'eligibles' has any by-blows. We want to be sure of the ability to reproduce," Mary added lightly, sliding one eye to glance at the rising color that again appeared on her chaperone's face.

Indeed, that lady's face had turned a strange combination of white, red, and purple, but her voice was level as she responded stiffly, "Just as you wish." She started to move away, causing Mary to laugh aloud and reach out to hold her back.

"I know you wouldn't truly, but I'll spare you the effort of trying to nonplus me," Mary said, squeezing the lady's arm affectionately.

"You must watch what you say, Miss, or one day I'll surprise you," Mrs. Pennett threatened.

Mary rolled her eyes playfully. "Ah, you and Mama! Here I am, an ancient, and yet I must pretend to be an ingenue."

"You never were that, but you can at least pretend not to be a scamp."

"The story of my life: I am neither fish nor fowl. Speaking of which, shall we go in to dinner?"

"Did no one sign up to escort you?" Mrs. Pennett asked, mildly miffed at every gentleman in the room for ignoring her darling.

"You know they did not. Come, you may take my arm instead."

"I will not. Let us elect some fellow, that you may charm him over the pudding," Mrs. Pennett said briskly, casting an eye about the room, assessing the unoccupied fellows. Under her breath she counted them off, muttering, "Too poor. Too ugly. Too fat. Too old. Stupid *and* ugly. Poor. Poor. Too young. Just plain silly . . . ah, there's a likely one! What do you say, Puss, shall we attach Mr. Everson?"

Mary turned to observe the man, though she had known him all her life. He was a hunting crony of her father's. He was, like herself, not exactly swimming in money, so the rumor mill said, but well enough off. It was obvious he liked the contents of his plate, for his form was gently rounded, but his was a kind and gentle nature, she knew. There was absolutely nothing of the Lancelot about him, but then neither was he the kind to be forward with a lady, so Mary answered with just the tiniest sigh, "Yes, let us attack dear Mr. Everson."

"I said 'attach,' not 'attack'."

"Yes, but my word is the more accurate, I believe," Mary said, pasting a smile upon her lips as they approached their target.

When dinner was over, Mary coaxed Mr. Everson into a dance. She did not point out the gravy stain on his cravat, nor did she lose her smile when he stepped on her toes. She also winced only a little when his lisped and hasty compliment at the end resulted in a slight spray from his lips upon her person. She did not jump too far when he tried to wipe the dots of spittle from her shoulder, and she did not beg off when he asked to sign her program for a second dance later in the evening. The only thing she did to show her true responses was to shudder slightly when his warm, wet lips actually penetrated her glove and left a sticky mark on the back of her hand. But perhaps he took the motion as a compliment, for his watery eyes were glittering when he bowed himself away.

Mrs. Pennett joined her charge swiftly, a pained look on her face. "Was it unbearable?" she asked quietly.

"Oh, yes," Mary said. Then she sighed, "No, I guess not. I have given him another dance." She shuddered again, then turned to the lady. "Remind me, Gladys. Do I really want to find a husband this badly?"

"Yes, Puss, you really do."

"I was afraid of that."

"Let's find another candidate, shall we?"

Mary nodded, closing her eyes for a moment. It was so humiliating that she was despairing enough to come to this point. How graceless! How lowering! That she must shop for a husband as coldly as she would for candles! But there was nothing for it. She could go on living with her parents until they were dead and gone, or she could make this effort to change her life. Children, she must remember children. They would be her compensation for a less than perfect arrangement.

When she opened her eyes Mrs. Pennett was gone, already stalking some poor creature for her charge to pester, no doubt. Mary stood where she was for a minute, surveying the dancers, seeing the batting eyes and attentive heads that spoke volumes on the matter of interest, or at least flirtation. Young faces, all of them full of promise.

Of a sudden, she felt the hair on the back of her neck stand up, and slowly she turned her head from the scene before her, with the queer and unmistakable feeling that she was being observed. She gazed into the darkness of the colonnaded hallway behind her, unable to see for a moment until her eyes adjusted to the lack of illumination. A tingle of not-quite-fear went up her spine, until finally she located a pair of shining eyes peering at her out of the darkness. The being moved, and she made out the fact that he was etching her a bow, saying not a word in greeting.

In her turn, she dipped into a curtsy. She was not

13

startled, though a little unnerved perhaps, for if she chose to think along a fanciful line, it would be easy to believe she was in the presence of a silent and perhaps not quite friendly spirit.

But the spell was broken as the being moved forward, becoming corporeal in the light shed from the candles above the dancers.

"Ah!" she said aloud as she recognized him.

"You know me, madam? You have the advantage," spoke the Blade, his ginger-colored lashes blinking once over seemingly impossibly light blue eyes.

"You are the Duke of Rothayne," she said, for he was so breathtakingly beautiful that she needed to hear herself say his name just to make him seem more a man than a spirit. She found herself standing a little taller, noting in some part of her brain that she was then nearly as tall as his chin, and finally she managed to add, "And I am Lady Wagnall."

He put out his hand. A little clumsily she offered her own. He shook it, his grip strong but not brutish.

After a moment she realized that she had been staring at him, silently marveling at his voice when he had spoken. It was exactly what she would have it be, for it was deep and resonant and purring, the voice of a stage villain, the devil in angel's clothing. And she had left her hand in his all the time she stared at him. Belatedly she withdrew her hand, burying it self-consciously in the folds of her skirts.

"Is there some way I may assist you?" she asked. She thought it sounded a little stupid, but he was just staring at her, and it was hard to think clearly with those blue eyes boring into hers.

He gave a small chuckle, and leaning toward her a little so that his features were picked out by the candlelight in a somewhat eerie fashion, said, "You would not ask such a question if you knew me better."

At first she was confused by his response, but then a stain of color touched her cheeks, for she very much had the impression that he was not speaking in any kind of proper connotation.

"Your grace?" she said uncertainly.

"Lady Wagnall, I must inform you that I overheard your conversation with your companion."

She blushed anew.

"You are seeking a husband."

She stared at him, her eyes closing just a little as she nearly frowned, her lower lip coming out just slightly. It would be easy to deny, for if he was any sort of gentleman, he would accept whatever she chose to say. But, too, there was that about him which compelled honesty. It must be his knack of not blinking.

He waited for her to take either path open to her: denial, or coquetry. Why not himself for a husband, since that was what she sought? Why not flutter those long eyelashes, say some clever thing, try to fix his attention? It was exactly what ninety out of a hundred ladies in the situation would do, and the ten remaining would boldly lie to his face and expect him to accept it.

Finally, under the assessing weight of those sky-blue eyes, she said, simply, "Yes."

He blinked slowly, striving not to reveal his astonishment. She had taken neither of the well-worn paths he anticipated, but had cut her own, by virtue of simply admitting the truth.

He smiled then, and she felt her eyes grow wide again, for he was magnificent, simply magnificent when he smiled. "Ah, good. We may be friends," he said, continuing to smile slightly.

"Your grace?" she stammered out again.

"I like honest people, Lady Wagnall. I cannot abide liars. I appreciate the honor bestowed upon me when you bothered to tell me the truth."

"I always tell the truth," she said breathlessly. She then gave herself a mental shake, drew her eyes away from his, and said to the air, "What a pleasure it was to meet you, your grace." She made as if to leave, but he did not move out of her way, causing her to pause awkwardly.

"I must assume it was indeed your pleasure, for you just told me you always tell the truth." His eyes glittered down at her, forcing her at last to look back into his face.

"You are the strangest man," she said without really meaning to.

He laughed then. "And that, too, is the truth. No, don't leave just yet. I have not had the opportunity to etch my name upon your program."

With awkward hands she surrendered her card to him, and saw him write across one line simply the name 'Godfrey'.

"Godfrey," she found her mouth moving yet again, seemingly without being connected to her brain. "It's from the Old German. It means 'divinely peaceful'."

He lifted one cinnamon eyebrow and asked with a sardonic edge, "You are a student of names, Lady Wagnall? Tell me then, in your esteemed knowledge, does the appellation suit the bearer, or not?"

"Oh, you are certainly divine," she said, staring straight into his handsome face as though something physically compelled her to do so. "But I sincerely doubt that you are the slightest bit peaceful."

He laughed again as he handed her back her program, his smile going all the way to his eyes. Suddenly she was smiling too, for he was irresistible in his amusement.

"My lady, it was my very great pleasure to meet you tonight," he said, giving her a shallow bow that

16

brought his face very near hers. Only then did he step back enough so that she could pass.

She stepped past him, but then she turned back slowly. "I wonder, is that true? Was it a pleasure? Do you also never tell lies, your grace?"

"No, my dear, I tell them all the time. I am, alas, entirely wicked."

Her head quirked a little to one side, taking in the fact that his face was now strangely blank and his voice was no longer filled with hidden laughter.

They seemed frozen that way for a moment. Incredibly, she sensed a hesitation in him, or was it perhaps a regret? Could it be that he was waiting for her renouncement, for her censure?

"I already knew that, from the very first moment I saw you," she said over her shoulder, just before she turned her back to him and walked quietly away.

His laughter followed her and rang in her ears until Mrs. Pennett came up and whisked her away to yet another unendurable dance match.

As he watched the lady walk away, Godfrey's laughter faded, and he leaned back against the colonnade, crossing his arms over his chest. It was a familiar pose, filled as it was with self-containment and the flavor of ready rebuff, which he adopted automatically as soon as it occurred to him that for a moment he had shown the lady his true face. Not "The Blade's" cynical, rakish face, nor the social face he wore that requested a dare or a challenge that might be met. Not even the controlled sneer he used to fully quash those who presumed upon his tolerance. No, for a moment he had allowed the anguished, wounded side—the side of his nature he often pretended was firmly buried—to reach his features. The event was startling, for it was the first

17

time he had ever done so, especially with a woman, since years past. Easy to show interest in a woman's charms, yes. Pleasure, even passion, but *never* this secret side of his soul, for it was a truth that one could not pierce a target if one could not find it. He had long since learned that women could be fickle, and long since concluded that his was not a nature that should be allowed to love. He had loved twice, and very unwisely. He would never do so again. Women were for dalliance only. Marriage was unthinkable. If the protective guards — his sharp tongue, his cutting ways, his lack of fidelity to anyone — had earned him the nickname "The Blade", then all to the better. It was exactly the way he wanted it.

And yet, this rather ordinary woman had made him forget his poise for a moment. He frowned, wondering how it had happened. No doubt it was the fact that he had not expected her honest answer to his observations of her matrimonial ambitions. He was, after all, still capable of finer feelings, and she had been graceful enough to give him the truth when he demanded it, instead of denials or flirtation. It was her unaccustomed forthrightness that had thrown him off kilter for a moment, allowing his emotions rather than his habitual manner to come to the fore.

Or perhaps it was the assessment in her eyes that had discomfited him, a trace of knowledge that spoke of his most recent escapade, the common knowledge of his sins. There was no way to explain, to deny, that, yes, he had met with Lady Peddy in the cemetery, but contrary to popular rumor, had not committed any carnal act with her there. He had taken her to a hotel, mindful of her comfort as well as his own.

He was used to disapproval — he did what he liked, societal censure being an old, wearied song he scarce heard anymore — but the remarkable thing was that the assessment he had seen in Lady Wagnall's eyes had not been one of disapproval. He had seen amusement there, and frank curiosity, and even something rather like reception. Now *that* he was no longer used to! Acceptance, yes, for he was a wealthy duke and was therefore welcome company regardless of his reputation, but an actual sense of *reception,* no. The difference being, he said to himself in something like amazement, that one would merely allow his presence, while the other welcomed it.

Despite his secret sorrows, Godfrey was not a somber man. Lady Wagnall, whether meaning to or not, had amused him, even pleased him. Despite himself, he recognized the growing feeling in his chest to be no less than that of *liking.* There were those in the world who knew him better than the gathered crowd, and who therefore would not have been so very surprised to see him smiling softly to himself. They might well have been pleased to note that there was neither self-derision nor even his more usual contempt, in that beautiful smile.

Godfrey made the usual rounds, securing with little more than a nod and a murmured word a time to meet one Mrs. Trimball following this festivity for one of their own devising. She was a fetching baggage, a little common in a way that seemed to be her best charm, and he knew from practical experience that hers were warm and inviting arms. A pity, in a way—but, no, not really— that soon he would meet with her no more. He would pass out of her arms just as he had the arms of every other female he had bedded in the past fifteen years. He could have arranged that they leave earlier, but he did not care to leave so soon. He had signed his name to Lady Wagnall's card, and was surprised to find that he truly wished to keep that assignation. He gave a small mental shrug, explaining to

19

himself that there were a variety of pleasures to be had in the world, and he could not think of a reason to deny himself the simple one of a country dance. A dance with someone he *liked*. Mrs. Trimball would wait, for he found he did not like the idea of standing up Lady Wagnall.

Chapter Two

In the past three weeks the weather had changed abominably. What had been a rather pleasant stretch of summer-like weather in May had left no one prepared for the howling, slashing, dripping, positively dreary and endless rainstorm that had followed. Ladies even took to not bothering to put on their hats until they were safely inside a building, for otherwise it was either snatched from their heads, or else it was tugged to and fro, putting all their hairdressers' work to nothing. Satin slippers were put away, replaced by hardier pattens or half-boots that would not be spoiled three feet outside one's front door, and parasols were flatly forgotten for they were ludicrous under the circumstances. Parties were cancelled due to flooded roads, and in one case the flooding of the hostess's home. Engagements for fetes were rearranged time and again, until finally they were simply cancelled altogether. It looked as though it would rain forever, and the entire city of London was completely glum about it.

"We must *do* something," Mary's brother, Randolph, had declared one gray, overcast morning. He sat slumped in the wing chair before the fire, but his eyes were turned to the window as though he were mesmerized by the patter of rain against the glass. Speaking slowly, heavily, his eyes fixated, he had repeated, "We must do *something,* or else I shall go mad."

"In that case it may be too late already," Mary said, grinning at her sister over their brother's head.

"No, he's right, Mary. We," declared Lydia firmly, "must have a party. But what kind of party? I vow another ball is not the answer. How many times can one say the same things to the same set of people in the same circumstances?"

"Oh yes, changing the circumstances does make all the comments seem quite new, does it not?"

"Mary," Randolph said heavily. "Stop being a ninny-hammer, and consider the problem at hand."

His wife, Elsbeth, looked up from her stitchery long enough to nod agreement with her husband.

"I wish I could stretch my legs a bit," Lydia's husband, Sedgwick, said. "I feel as though I've been living in a box for days on end."

"Yes, we could all use with a little exercise," Lydia agreed.

"Can't exactly ride to the hounds now," Randolph put in gloomily.

"Oh yes we could," Mary said slowly as a thought occurred to her. Her voice started to rise as she began to fill with enthusiasm at her own idea. "You can do anything inside you can do outside, if only you change things 'round a bit."

"Never say you mean to bring horses in on the Aubusson rugs?" Elsbeth cried.

"Yes, that's quite what I mean, only the horses I am thinking of must be only a few inches high."

The siblings and spouses looked at one another, and despite their initial resistance, a house party was born that day.

They received a quick response of enthusiastic acceptance from nearly every soul that was invited, and within a week the event was upon them. It was declared by a large banner just inside the door that it was to be a "Hounds Day." The guests drew slips of numbered paper from a bowl as they entered, forming miscellaneous groups of "riders" by virtue of matching numbers. Mary led them into the ballroom, where she stood upon a chair to deliver her instructions.

"It is all very simple: I shall play the part of the hounds by reading the first clue. After that, it is up to you to 'follow the hounds', or in other words to locate the items that you have been instructed to find. Recall your group's number, stay together and work as a team, and do not follow the clues that were numbered and intended for other groups. If you do, you forfeit the hunt. When you find each of your intended items, bring them back to this room, and our good man Pendleton there will mark it upon the score board here." She pointed up at the large graph pinned to the wall, in front of which stood their butler, Pendleton. The graph was lined with a number of 'lanes', one for each group of hunters, at the start of which posed a cut out drawing of a horse.

"I say," called one of the guests in group number five, "Our nag there isn't a very handsome fellow, is he?"

Everyone laughed, and despite their prompting Mary said she must refuse to tell who the artist had been, though she did say, "He would not care to have his artistry laughed upon." Whereupon all eyes turned to Randolph, for he had flushed in a telltale manner. He flushed even more and laughed at the same time, receiving the slaps upon his back and loud guffaws with good grace. "Fellow's name is Eye of the Beholder" he said with a grin.

That was met with more laughter. Mary went on to explain that there would be prizes for first, second, and third place for 'bagging the fox', that is, reaching the end of the graph, and that a luncheon for all would follow the end of the game. When those in the gathering were done murmuring their appreciation, she produced a slip of paper, from which she read:

> "Travel not to the out of doors,
> For no prizes will then be yours.
> Seek, then, inside to find your clues,
> The first: Each hour I pay my dues."

She then raised a horn to her lips for a brief and discordant blast, and with a loud shout of 'Tally-Ho!' the room broke into pandemonium. Some fled the room at once, others stood about discussing the meaning of the clue, which most easily agreed must be some kind of clock, and still others moved off stealthfully, as though they truly would startle a fox from some hidden place.

Mary and her family came together except for her mother, who was already hurrying the servants into arranging the ballroom into a space for serving the luncheon. The siblings giggled and whispered, and applauded when the first groups returned with their 'huntings' in hand.

"Darling," their mother called in passing.

All heads turned, for she could mean any one of them.

"See what the stir at the front door is all about, please," she instructed as she glided by, a dripping candelabra in each hand.

Mary was given the duty, this being deemed the 'privilege' of being the only offspring who still resided at home. As she stepped into the foyer it was to see one of the footmen receiving Lord Rothayne's topcoat and hat. "Your grace!" she called. She had known he was to be invited, but when there had been no response she had assumed that such a Corinthian had no need to amuse himself at such a countrified party as they had proposed.

His smile was genuine, telling her that he had not immediately forgotten her after they had shared that one dance nearly a month ago. He had flirted outrageously with her then, and even though she had known it was all in sport, she blushed a little at the sight of him, recalling how much and how freely she had laughed while in his arms.

"Forgive the intrusion, my lady, but I have been at a friend's hunting box and only saw the invitation this morning. I decided to play my chances and see if I would be admitted, despite being not only unexpected but tardy as well," he said blithely.

"Of course you are welcome, though you have missed some of the fun already. Here, draw a number and we shall unite you with your group of fellow huntsmen," she said, presenting the bowl to him. She forced herself to blink, for as she had that first time they met, she now found herself staring at his great good looks.

He drew a number two from the bowl. "Ah, my favorite number."

"Is it?" she asked, making a motion to indicate he should follow her.

"Yes, one and one. Just the way I like it."

She came to a stop, staring at him. He had spoken in an intimate, familiar way, rather suggestively. He had done that before, she recalled.

And again that sheltered look came over his face.

She stared at him, unblinking. "Your grace," she finally said slowly, "Do you speak thusly to all of your acquaintances?"

"No," he said rather curtly. Here he was again, discomfited. Yes, it definitely had something to do with her genuine pleasure as she received him. "I am downright nasty to the ones I do not care for."

She shook her head slightly. "We are friends, then, I take it? Although we scarcely know one another?"

He took a deep breath, staring off into the distance as though making an assessment, but when he looked back at her his features were clear. "Yes, I should like to think we became instant friends."

"And you will continue to speak naughtily and in double entendres?"

"Yes," he said, grinning now, completely unabashed.

One moment he was all openness, teasing, light, and the next he was shut away, as though someone had just closed the shutters against the sun, and then the reverse again. It was nothing less than intriguing. More than that, it tugged in some curious way at Mary's heart.

"All right then," she said, smiling at last. "Just so we both understand that this is your way. I will not take offense, if you will not mean what you say."

"I always mean what I say, however fleetingly."

"Well then, that you do not *act* upon what you say."

"Yes," he laughed then, obviously and genuinely pleased with her. "Since you are to be my friend, I could agree to that." He held up a finger. "One stipulation, though. You already have been warned, from my own lips, that I am thoroughly unrepentant of my evil inclinations. Though I would never touch one finger to one hair upon your head without your approval, I will always do my best to persuade you to join me willingly in my debaucheries. My life is dedicated to self-satisfaction, and I am very much afraid that I must have the freedom to at least attempt my goals via my persuasive and provocative comments." There, he had just put this relationship on a level where he could be comfortable, full of humor and lightness.

"And were those persuasive and provocative comments the reason you left England for a while?" she dared to ask openly. If he could be so blunt,

26

then she must be accorded the same privilege.

"Exactly so. It seems that Prinny did not care over-much for my observation that his father ought to have had a mistress or two, to spare the Queen, you see."

Mary raised a hand to her mouth, covering a startled sound that was half a laugh. It may very well be joked about that the mad King's poor queen ought to be the mad one, having had the exclusive attentions of her husband—fifteen children's worth in fact—but it was not the sort of thing that one wanted one's Regent to know one had said.

"And now you are pardoned?"

He shrugged. "Or perhaps agreed with, do you think?"

She shook her head, amazed at his forthrightness, but she refused to be nonplussed. "So, in the matter of our 'relationship', you are saying you must be allowed a free tongue, and that I am to be allowed the right to for-evermore laugh and say 'no'."

"Quite."

"But why?" she cried, spreading hers hands as though asking an impossibly obscure question.

"Because I like you." It was amazingly true, as soon as it came from the half-hidden depths of his brain, past his consciousness, and onto his lips. He went on quickly, hiding his own astonishment from himself, "You are the only young female I know who has not run from me screaming, rapped upon my person with an as-sortment of fans or lorgnettes, nor scolded me for my wicked tongue. I have been completely free with you, and all you do is laugh and let me please myself. It is an extraordinary pleasure, one I cannot, no, will not fore-swear, because I know you will not disappoint me by suddenly turning missish."

For the first time in her life, Mary was glad she was plain to look upon. Here was the most handsome man

27

in the world, telling her he liked her. She knew with certainty that such frankness would not have been possible if she had been in any way the sort of beauty with which one flirted. Such was his reputation: he could only befriend and speak so boldly to an unpretty girl. And she had no doubt it was mere friendship he sought. She was not quite sure why she knew this, though perhaps it was something in the way he held himself, but it was communicated silently to her as clearly as though he had spoken of it, whether he had consciously recognized it or no. Instead of being cast down by the sudden insight, she felt the exhilaration of being truly *seen* as a person worthy of liking. She felt quite overwhelmed for a moment, but she dare not disappoint him by doing exactly as he had forbade her: turning missish. Instead she clasped her hands together as though in prayer, and giving a stage sigh, replied with a smile, "Very well then, your grace. I grant you leave to be as naughty as you care to be, though my stipulation is that it must be for my ears alone. I have a reputation to maintain, you must know. However, the burning of my own ears is a small enough price to pay to claim such a wild creature as my friend."

He moved toward her, his hands clasped behind his back, his blue eyes as clear and sparkling as ice. He cast aside the unexpected sense of gratification her agreement had given him, unaccustomed as he was to anything other than physical relief with a woman, resorting to a more normal manner of address. He towered over her, very deliberately intimidating in his presence, to say, "Yes, my dear lady, I *am* a wild creature. Let us never forget that."

"And s-so, our friendship already begins," she said, stumbling over the words just a little as she moved away from him, half-turning, and only daring a quick glance over her shoulder to indicate that he was to follow her.

She brought him to his party of hunters, and then excused herself, claiming she would give away the clues if she stayed to hear the debates. In truth, she simply needed to move out of the sphere of the overwhelming Duke Rothayne, to let her pulse return to normal and to try and arrange her thoughts into a less chaotic pattern.

She stared out a window, unnoted by her family who were arguing back and forth concerning the arrangement of a bowl of flowers, until Mrs. Pennett tapped her on the shoulder. She jumped, causing the lady to ask, "Now what's on your mind then, Miss Mary, to make you so jittery?"

"To be honest," Mary replied, for she might as well not bother to try and hide much from her companion, who had an uncannily keen eye anyway, "I am thinking about Lord Rothayne."

"Oo, it would never do to get attached to that one, Puss," Mrs. Pennett said, wagging a finger.

"Well, of course it would not. He is the most unsuitable fellow imaginable, especially for my goals. No, it is not a thought of an alliance—let alone marriage—with him that disturbs me." She turned to look at her companion, suddenly finding a hedging statement coming from her lips, "It seems he wishes to be my friend, and just that. I have never had a gentleman friend before, and I was puzzling out how one goes about it."

"Pretty much the same as with a female, if you're really just friends," Mrs. Pennett said warily, with a glimmer in her eye which bespoke volumes of disapproval.

"Yes, I suspect you're right. What a goose I am," Mary said smoothly, slipping her arm through her companion's to lead her toward the kitchens to check on the progress of the forthcoming meal. She did not, would not explain that, yes, indeed it was not the thought of marrying Lord Rothayne that disturbed her—the very thought was absurd! No, it was rather the sudden, desolate and disconsoling thought that she knew she must marry some fellow who was not the least bit like him.

A huge cheer went up, shared by all, celebrating the winners of the Hounds Day. The sport had been the very thing to lift the gloom the weather had cast over them all, and the guests were uniformly so pleased as to be generous in their congratulations. Along one wall was a collection of items: a comb, a stocking, a pocketwatch, a feather, and about a hundred other bits and pieces of the household, the bounty that had been acquired in the hunt for clues. Team number six had won, having been the first to decipher correctly that the final clue meant they must find their corresponding number on the bottom of a shoe of a member of the household. Poor Mrs. Brumbold, the cook's assistant, had blushed furiously when she was dragged from the kitchens and made to present the bottom of her shoe as proof before the laughing crowd. This display was followed only a minute later when Elsbeth was proved to have the number four on her shoe, and Pendleton's shoe brought third place success to team number one. It was roundly applauded when the first prize turned out to be new and gaudily-made house slippers for the entire team — representative, after a fashion, of the final clue that had won the day for them — eclipsing the more ordinary haircombs, buckles, fans, and tobacco pouches that made up prizes for the ladies and gentlemen of the second and third places.

Mary's mother, Lady Cornelia, led the way in to luncheon upon the arm of her husband, Bertram. As their guests discovered that the meal was not to be formally consumed, but instead served in a buffet manner as a kind of pretense at *al fresco* dining, Mary flitted among them, gaily bestowing the less-than-artistic cut-out paper horses upon the members of the winning team. Her efforts caused yet more of the good humor that the day had brought, and she was eagerly summoned from one group to the next as they demanded someone be given their due as well. When she came to the group that included the Duke of Rothayne, it, alas, held no one of the winning team, but she offered other consolation by smiling in mock regret at her guests. "Worse luck!" she cried, for they had not only been last, but had missed a deal of the gaiety, so absorbed were they in their efforts to solve the clues.

"Oh, not really," Lord Avery said, his youthful face shining. "It was a jolly good time, don't you know."

"Yes, it was, wasn't it?" Mary beamed.

"I, for one, am thankful to *not* have a new pair of house slippers," the Duke spoke up, causing the others to laugh with appreciation. He balanced a china plate upon one hand, a fork in the other with which he served selected tidbits to himself.

Mary gave him a smile mixed with a silent sigh, for she was, she knew with a repeat of the day's sudden insight, quite besotted with the fellow, for now she was thinking that he even chewed beautifully. Such a graceful creature, but with the heart of a lion: all-devouring, self-satisfying, unconcerned with his own image. Perhaps besotted was not the right word; he was just such a foreign being, the like of which she had not met before. Foreignness was very attractive—that is why people cared to travel. But 'foreign' was just that: foreign. The traveler always returned home, seeking the comfort of the familiar. She knew very well that he was the very opposite model of the man whom she must find and marry.

"Those slippers were simply atrocious, weren't they?" she asked the crowd, but she was looking at the Duke.

They all laughed again and agreed. The Duke laughed, too, and Mary had to laugh with him.

As it happened, the party was such a success that the guests lingered on. No dancing had been planned, but suddenly people were forming couples, and Lydia was pressed into playing the harpsichord for them all. Randolph brought out his french horn, and the brother and sister bravely struggled through ten tunes before they pleaded exhaustion. Lady Cornelia, fearful that she would soon be in a position where she would have to feed them all yet another meal, stood up to announce that Mary would sing and accompany herself on the harp, and then her other offspring would play one final tune to conclude the day's events.

Mary cast her mother a dark look, for it was not the first time that the lady had so blatantly found a way to display her unmarried daughter's charms, but the harm was already done. Moving to the one-step platform that graced one corner of the ballroom, she pulled the cover from the harp, settled herself with as much poise as she could muster, and strummed the strings to find that she was satisfied with the tuning of the instrument.

She sang "When the Heart Doth Wing to Heav'n," and felt she only played one wrong note and that her voice had been up to the complicated tune reasonably well. She looked out upon the applauding crowd, but it was only the Duke's quiet clapping, accompanied as it was by appreciative eyes, that meant anything to her. He would not give her Spanish coin: his applause was sincere. She blushed a little, and nodded her head becomingly in acknowledgement of the praise.

The Duke looked upon the somewhat less than pretty lady, and then around at the forty-odd people that remained assembled to hear the final tune to be given by Mary Wagnall's siblings. To himself he thought with a sudden, unexpected clarity: *But what a great lot of fools they are not to realize the pearl inside the oyster that is Lady Mary Wagnall!* Yet it was obvious just from the looks on their faces, that most had dismissed Mary Wagnall the moment she had ceased singing. It was seldom that one met a genteel lady who had been raised to demonstrate the merest intelligence, let alone this one's tolerance and humor and exquisite manners. That she could sing so prettily was as icing upon a cake. The Duke, looking at the scene with eyes quite different than they would have been yesterday, watched as Mary rose and bowed, as she walked back to join the crowd as though on water, a gliding graceful step that displayed her womanly curves to advantage and emphasized the tidy waistline. Her laugh was almost as musical as her singing voice, and he knew with an unexpected simplicity that it was a desire to hear that laugh again that had brought him here this day. There were some things that could not be denied, not even by an old rogue like himself: if ever a soul shone brightly, it was hers. As she had looked directly upon him to solicit his approval, he had felt a curious, extraordinary glow of warmth that she thought him worthy of her friendship.

Oh, but look at these dolts, every one of them blind, he continued to himself. That the physically imperfect, yet radiantly wonderful Lady Wagnall was reduced to drubbing amongst them for a husband was really a pity almost beyond enduring.

Well, as strange as it was for him to have a woman who was in truth a friend and not a lover, he and she had come to an almost immediate and curiously comfortable accord, and it was by virtue of that newfound and oddly cherished accord that he gave himself instantaneous permission to assist the lady into finding someone worthy of her.

Oh, never himself, of course, never. *He* knew better

33

than anyone that he was not worthy, but he had the sense to know who was, and he was in the position to bring those fellows into the lady's circle. It would mean attending some truly horrendous routs—stifling, boring, and dreadfully restrictive—but for the sake of his newest friend, he would do it. The Duke lived for himself, but part of that self included a devotion to the rare few whom he could call 'friend'.

His was the last pair of hands to cease clapping, and the fact was noted in whispers behind a few fans. Ah well then, he noted at once, he must hurry this lady into marriage with another if he was to have a chance to remain her friend, before any attentions of his should stain her reputation unalterably and to the worse.

With that thought in mind, he moved to be the first to leave. He thanked his hostess for including him and for disregarding his tardy arrival, and thanked his host for 'an intriguing new sport', and finally gave his hand to the lady with whom he would have preferred to stay and chat amiably, but for whose sake he must leave.

"I am so glad you could come, your grace," she said warmly, well aware of the suddenly erratic pulse that beat through the fingers which he clasped in his shapely hand. His blue gaze had an intensity that she seemed to note more and more as time passed.

"As am I. You must promise to sing again for me sometime."

She lowered her eyes a little in genuine confusion as to how to answer the warm words, and when she raised them again, she found herself saying giddily and playfully, "At Almacks, do you think?"

"That would be delightful. You sing as do the angels above."

"I daresay the patronesses would not think so, if I should happen to start warbling upon that hallowed ground."

34

"Then perhaps you should sing for me privately. An angel should be singing in heaven, and I declare I could take you there." His fingers tightened on hers, and if he had pulled just a little she would have been forced to come up against his length.

She laughed then, back on ground that seemed less shaky. His regard was too unnerving, but this playful waywardness was becoming familiar. "Rogue!" she called him, squeezing his hand back, hard.

"Admit it, you do not mind in the slightest my proposals." His blue eyes glowed like diamonds as he removed his hand and flexed it, as though it had gone numb, just for her benefit, just to hear her laugh again.

"The thing I *do* mind is learning that I must be nearly as corrupted as yourself, to let you go on so."

"Ah, there is hope then. Lady Wagnall *is* corruptible. On that note, I shall say my good nights, my dear lady." So saying, he bent long enough to press the lightest kiss upon the back of her hand, and then bowed himself out of her life for the next week.

Chapter Three

When he walked back into her life, it was to be while she was tending the garden in the lightest rain to date. Compared to how it had been falling in massive quantities for days, the light misting of today seemed almost summer-like, and she found herself drawn to the out of doors. She had no idea how long he had stood silently observing her, but when she turned to pull the weed bucket closer, she was startled to find a pair of water-dotted hessians beside it.

Once her eyes had risen past the sartorial splendor—despite the light rain—of his morning clothes to finally recognize his face, she began to struggle at once from her knees. "Your grace!" she cried.

He reached down and caught her elbow, assisting her as she rose. With an amused lift of one eyebrow, he quipped, "Did I startle you?", knowing full well that he had.

"Of course," was her somewhat crisp reply as she snatched off her tattered half-handers and made a few pointless efforts at wiping her fingers on the cloth tied from a string at her waist. "You quite surprised me. Did no one bring you from the house?"

"I never entered the house, so you must not blame your staff. In fact, I walked today, and so did not even have the grace to leave a carriage in the drive. So you see, we are quite unnoted, and quite alone."

She reached to adjust the sun bonnet on her head, drops scattering, hoping the movement would cover the fact that she was a little flustered to be found in her worst and oldest gown, with mud about her fingertips, and hearty half-boots peeping out beneath the sodden and too-short hem. That he would make suggestive remarks only seemed to point up the fact that she was atrociously adorned this day.

"You walked! In this rain? Well, I suppose it is no more extraordinary than that I should be out mucking about in the mud. I am, however, grateful to you that you did not bring others with you, for I should hate to have to make my curtsies to any callers looking as I do."

"Yes, well, 'tis a curious costume. Do you not have the means to employ a gardener?" he drawled with a comically disdainful set to his mouth.

"Three in fact. But this little patch is all mine." She turned to regard the muddy spot where she had been closely placing starter plants in the seemingly vain hope of someday seeing sunshine. "Mama and I have quite different tastes in flowers, and she allowed me this little bit of earth to do with as I please, as it is at the back of the house. I began discussing what I wanted here with the head gardener, but then I found I had an interest in it myself, and so it has become my pet project."

"But, my dear, I do not see one rose amongst your selections," he drawled. She might have wondered at that, but he did not. It was the essence of what had drawn him here to her side today: she was not as other English Roses, that is to say, ladies. She was not conventional, nor predictable, nor afraid to say a

37

word or two of her own thoughts. She was the freshness of the wild rose in the domestic patch—others
would pretend not to see her there, but he could only
admire her cheekiness at being something other than
she ought.

"Not a one. I like the wilder flowers, the ones with
exuberant colors and unrefined scents, though
Mama finds it all somewhat shameful, I believe."

At that he gave a knowing chuckle, and said, "I
believe it is a Mama's duty to find many things
shameful."

"I daresay you are right, this conversation being
among them, no doubt," she grinned at him, finally
relaxing a little under the effects of his charm.
Stooping quickly to scoop up the weed bucket, she
began to walk across the freshly-scythed lawn. He
followed a step or two behind. "What brings you this
day, your grace?" she asked over her shoulder.

"I have a dozen intriguing answers to that, dearest
Lady Wagnall, but I will not burden you with them
right now. I actually came in earnest, to speak with
you. It seems we are very good friends, and yet we
know almost nothing of one another." He paused,
and then said, "You know I overheard your conversation with your chaperone. I know of your desire to
wed. I am desirous of helping you to that end."

Her steps slowed, and her lips parted slightly in
shock before she snapped them shut, blinking several
times in astonishment. "I . . . I don't know what to
say—"

"I could say some things for you: 'Why is he doing
this? What sort of rackety fellow does he think to
attach to me? How dare he interfere in my life
this way?' Am I close to being correct? Isn't that
much of what you are thinking?" he asked, one eye-

brow perched rather archly.

" 'Tis exactly what I would be thinking if any other had said such a thing," she said tentatively. "But now I do not denounce you and bid you leave because I believe *you,* particularly you, are making a sincere — albeit curious — proposal."

"Quite sincere. But why do you call it curious?"

She spread her hands wide, the weed bucket swinging, as she cried in embarrassment, "Well, look at me! Why should you care what becomes of such a one as myself? I could understand if I were a great beauty —"

He cut her off abruptly, " 'Tis very true, Mary, that 'beauty is as beauty does', so I'll have none of that nonsense. You wish to marry. I wish to be your friend. I find I wish it very greatly, and friendship is not dependent on beauty, as I can well tell you." For a moment his voice had grown embittered, but then he seemed to mentally shake himself, and went on, "Friends help friends, and if I happen to introduce you to the lucky man who finally wins you, then he will be perhaps a little less likely to forbid my presence in your home. You see, once again I am only serving myself."

He turned a little away from her, idly kicking at pieces of grass that had been missed by the scythe and left too long. He continued, "I have pledged to 'get thee wed' and yet I have no notion of what kind of fellow you are looking for."

Mary came to a halt, causing him to stop as well. She dragged a hand across her cheek which had become wet in the misty rain, and gave a large sigh, her face reflecting the turmoil of the unnamed and impossible emotions she felt within. "I find such a conversation awkward at best, but since I believe what you say, and I find I desire your matrimonial assistance—since my own effort has proved most pathetic—I do not doubt it is worth our time to hold such a conversation nonetheless."

His head twisted inquiringly on his graceful neck. "Do you not know by now that all our conversations are meant to be awkward?"

The abused expression fell from her face, replaced by a bittersweet smile as she laughed, the rain running from the top of her bonnet to splash off her shoulders.

"My dear girl, may I offer you my coat?" he inquired at once, for she wore none.

"No, no, I am only wet, not cold," she assured him. She sighed again, and resumed walking. This time he kept pace with her as she led them toward the tool shed. So, he had asked to assist her out of friendship, and the proof thereof was to have her describe her 'desired mate'. Well then, he should have what he asked for; she plunged in at once, before her mixed up feelings could choke back her ability to speak.

"What sort of fellow, you ask? Hmmm. Well, I'm sure I couldn't say exactly, but I do rather picture a quiet fellow, with a propensity toward reading, but he must be able to dance, at least a little." She smiled up at him finally, giving in to the humor that must go with this outlandish discourse. "He need not be taller than I, but I would prefer he not be too round. I should like him to have his own teeth, but hair is not essential."

"Ah, you describe a paragon," the Duke said drolly.

"He must not be a gambler, and must not smoke a pipe. Nasty things, pipes. Oh, and Mrs. Pennett and

I decided he should not be *too* old, as the main point is . . . is . . ." Her humor had led her too far, so that now words failed her, and she blushed a striking shade of scarlet.

"Is what, Mary, my love?" purred Godfrey.

"Well, I think you must know a lady of my advanced years is hopeful of offspring, and soon," she answered, hiding within primness, choosing just that moment to fling open the shed door and disappear inside.

He waited patiently without, his hands clasped behind his back, his well-shaped legs spread in a casual posture until finally she returned to his side.

"Would you come inside and take tea?"

"Nasty thing, tea," he echoed her earlier tone, shuddering eloquently. "Ah, Mary, do not look away from me. I have told you before that I do not wish to see you turn missish on me. That you want children makes all the sense in the world to me, your confidante and friend. Again, I tell you I far more appreciate your honesty than I ever would your blushes."

"I cannot help myself. Ladies and gentlemen do not speak of such things," she said, forcing herself to meet his gaze.

"Then let us, between the two of us, not be gentlepersons. Let us be a scamp and a rogue. It would be far easier, I assure you."

She nodded at once, her delicate frame straightening in subconscious acknowledgement. "You have the right of it. Indeed, I recall I already agreed to terms of this nature. You are right to not let me renege. Carry on, then, dear Duke Rothayne, for I shall not allow myself to blush ever again in your presence."

"A pity, that. I tell you, were I to strip naked before you, I should be most annoyed if you did *not* blush."

Her mouth quirked, but no reprimand came from her lips.

"Shall I tell you, then, that I have not been idle this past week? I have actually forced myself into a chair and given thought to the matter. I believe I have composed a very fine list, consisting of a dozen upstanding fellows who ought to have the good fortune to meet you. Shall we start tomorrow? Are you invited to Madam Frelorn's cotillion?"

"We are," she nodded, meaning her family as well as herself.

"Then I shall meet you there, and see that you are placed in the arms of a dozen eligibles."

She crossed her arms, not unlike a shield before her, and implored, "Please do not make it too obvious that I am headhunting."

"I shall not. I know full well that nothing would attract a fellow less," he said somewhat indignantly.

"Thank you," she murmured.

"I hope to arrange that you may make the acquaintance of one Mr. Charles Bretwyn."

"Whatever you think best," she said, indicating the direction of the house. They began to stroll again, heading toward the rear entrance.

"Good. You will like him. I like him myself, and that is a rare thing."

"Then no doubt I shall, too."

"You trust my judgement so far, then?" he asked, sidestepping a puddle, coming close to her side so that they were near enough to touch. She moved a little away, as though to give him room.

"Silly of me, I suppose, but yes, I do. I cannot think that you would bother to walk out in the rain just to place me in the middle of some complicated hoax. You tell me you are wicked, but you must not be entirely so, because I *do* trust you."

"Even the devil keeps his bargains," he said in a low voice, his eyes suddenly turned away to the horizon, his expression instantly remote.

"But he does not care, not about some silly little unwed woman. Not enough to help her find a measure of contentment in this world," she said, laying her hand upon his arm.

"You should not have done that," he said, turning his head to gaze down at her hand. His eyes then raised to hers. "Now that you have touched my arm, I shall feel free to touch yours."

"Terrible," she said with a smile.

"I am. Trust me in that also."

She laughed. He could change the course of a conversation so quickly, it baffled the mind. "I try, but sometimes you make it difficult to believe you are as awful as you claim."

He smiled then, and her stomach flipped, and she drew her hand away. Yes, perhaps she ought not to have done that.

He tucked in his chin for a moment, revealing that he had noted her withdrawal, but his voice was all that is cheerful as he said, "You know, you have not given me permission to use your Christian name. It seems very strange that we should be such bosom mates and yet I must refer to you only as 'Lady Wagnall'. You have my complete consent to call me Godfrey, or if you prefer you may call me 'my love'."

She shook her head even as she gave a quick, slightly wavering smile. His choice of words — perhaps because of her advanced state of 'maiden-aunt-dom' — had the effect of making her feel just a little tipsy. "Of course you have my permission."

"And . . . just what *is* your Christian name?" he asked, one hand rubbing his chin in an exaggerated gesture of perplexity.

Again she smiled, accompanied by a breathless, quick laugh. "Mary."

"Ah. Mary. Maria. The namesake of the Holy Virgin. Well, we will see that you do not follow that lady's suit, shan't we, for I swear the bridal bed has not long to await your visit, not with such a clever and resourceful fellow as myself on your side. I shall meet you tomorrow then? At the Frelorns's?"

"I shall try to find another dress to wear," she said with an equally cheery tone. If she did not sound completely carefree, she hoped he took no note of it.

"Please do," he answered drolly.

"And what of you, your grace? Do you desire that I should search among my acquaintances to find *you* a spouse as well?"

"No," he said calmly. "If it ever comes to that, I should much rather you place me in a vat of boiling oil. I would be content with such, but not with that other heinous fate."

She laughed. "And this is the man who means to see me wed?"

"I do. I have the advantage of clarity of vision, you see, for I keep myself well clear of the traps and tricks of the matrimonial waters. I am a gifted pilot who can guide you past the shoals of fortune hunters and callow brutes, into the safe harbor of domestic bliss."

She laughed again, for he had meant to make her laugh. She did not voice the thought that came to her that this man would indeed make a very fine pilot, or more likely a pirate.

They stopped short of the back doors, and he took his leave of her. She watched him walk away, the rain falling upon them both, he so graceful and collected that it seemed only the wetted surfaces of his beaver reflected nature's dewy caress, while her bonnet dripped onto her shoulders, staining the bodice of the inelegant frock even more than before, as she stood silent and still, soaked and strangely forlorn, and unable to do anything but stand and wish the whole world was different than it really was.

Mrs. Hummold and rose to her polite bow.

show more than a house the pleasure. "It is your own...

do to you that ... do upon my account.... money, but I do

Chapter Four

"Mary, this is Mrs. Hummold and this her brother, Mr. Bretwyn, acquaintances of long standing. Lettice, Charles, this is my very good friend, Lady Mary Wagnall," the Duke said in that deep purr that was his voice, a benign smile on his face as he made the introductions.

Mary offered her hand to them both. She noted that Mr. Bretwyn was the possessor of an attractive face — not beautiful like the Duke, but quite pleasant — and his handshake was firm. His palms were not sweaty, so an appreciative smile came to her lips as she murmured, "Mr. Bretwyn, how do you do?"

"Fine, I thank you. And yourself?"

"Very well."

"Mary, may I put my name to your program?" the Duke interjected.

She smiled at him as she handed him her card, but the flash in her eyes told him that he could have been more subtle. She knew she could not be above coercing the gentlemen into dancing with her, but that this was Godfrey's friend made it somehow a more painful process.

Once he had signed her card, and Mr. Bretwyn had failed to offer to do the same, Godfrey turned to

Mrs. Hummold and pressed the point by asking if she would grace him with a dance.

"I thank you for the honor, your grace, but I do not dance," she replied. She added in a tone that spoke of mild disapproval, "Indeed, neither does Charles."

"In truth?" the Duke asked as though in regret, even as he turned his body just a little to glance down at Mary. "And why is that?"

Mary held her breath, but Mrs. Hummold did not take offense at the direct question. In fact, she seemed just as aware of the Blade's reputation as any lady present, and just as willing to overlook it, at least on a social footing. It was true that the Duke's pockets were plump, but Mary suspected it was actually his charm—however wicked it sometimes was— that drew the ladies to him.

"Because I have a limb that often disapproves of the sport, and Charles, because he does not care to."

Charles nodded at her side, adding, "It's not that I can't. It's that I don't enjoy it much, and neither do the ladies when I step on their toes."

Mary felt a finger jab into her back as the Duke moved slowly behind her, looking about as though he were observing the crowd. She lifted her chin, hoping her slight jerk had not been noted, and cried at once, "Why, Mr. Bretwyn, I would not mind at all if you should happen to step on my toes."

Mrs. Hummold stared at her in an openly startled manner, forcing her to add hastily, "For I should be stepping on yours as well."

The stare turned into an approving smile, and the lady turned to her brother and said, "See? Here is one who is not daunted by a little inexperience. Go on, you two, a set is just forming. I shall inform—"

she glanced at Mary's program, "—Captain Rodgers that since he was tardy, the next dance shall have to be his."

"My thanks," Mary murmured. She gave a wide-eyed glance toward Godfrey as she was led to where the others assembled for a country dance, and was pleased to note that he appeared gratified at her 'spontaneous' performance. True to his word, Mr. Bretwyn managed to step on her toes, and so she made a point of stepping on his in turn, and was rewarded for her efforts with a bright smile.

To her utter amazement, Mary's card not only filled entirely, but also quickly. Though it was true that only a few of the names belonged to the young men who cut such wide swaths in the area of the ingenues, it was also true that there was not one over fifty years of age among those names on her card. They were all reasonably bright fellows, and none of them poor, at least as far as rumor knew. As the evening progressed, it became quite clear to her that the Duke's occasional absences from her side were spent in tracking down some of these fellows in their various dens. Some fellows had no doubt been persuaded to leave a card table, still others their cigarillos, and yet others their glasses of port. He had gone where she could not, bringing the older, less silly fellows from the males-only places they had thought safe and quiet, no doubt. And he, that clever Blade, had presented all these models of matrimonial material smoothly, not too overtly, not too embarrassingly, and he had made it quite clear that he himself had no designs on the lady by virtue of the very fact that he had presented her with twenty other partners. She could only marvel at his adroitness, and gave herself up to the pure and simple pleasure of being entertained by a throng of, if not exactly ad-mirers, at least respectful participants. She did not even mind when Mr. Everson once again claimed her for a dance, and when he spattered her gown yet again with spittle she merely shrugged and passed on into the arms of yet another fellow.

Mary was aware that although the Duke did all he could to see that she was well-partnered, he was not himself without a dance or two. He smiled at her occasionally as they passed one another on the floor, and made her laugh once with a broad leer that meant the abundant charms (more commonly known as décolletage) of the lady in his arms had not gone unnoticed. As the evening advanced, Mary was not unaware that his grace spent a rather long bit of time in the corner with that particular lady. Their laughter was mostly quiet, their actions largely circumspect, but nonetheless Mary felt a sense of relief when they at last parted. She told herself this was because she did not wish the Duke to be so shocking in his behavior as to cause him to have to remove his presence from the Beau Monde yet again. How could he help her if he was banished by polite society once more? She saw the Duke move on to another group of acquaintances, only really turning her attention back to her dance partner when she saw the group did not include any temptresses.

Halfway through the evening, it was the Duke who claimed her for the dance for which he had signed her program.

"Are you having a pleasant evening?"

"A most pleasant evening," she sighed happily.

The dance divided them, but when they came back together, he said, "Your cheeks are flushed. You are positively shining."

Despite her earlier promise to him to the contrary, she blushed, and felt a thrill of happiness run up through her middle, manifesting itself in the form of a bright smile. "I feel as though the evening has been arranged just for me," she said somewhat breathlessly.

"It has, by myself. You have made some admirers tonight, I hope you realize."

"Have I? Then your efforts have not been in vain."

"Mr. Bretwyn has suggested an outing. I have accepted on your behalf."

"Your grace, it is then indeed an evening of triumph, for Lord Revenshaven and Lt. Hargood have also solicited an outing! But which date did Mr. Bretwyn have in mind? I should hate for my attempts at social success to all fall to nothing because they were arranged for the same day."

He looked down into her flushed and radiant face, and felt a smile reach up from somewhere deep inside his chest to touch his lips. She was happy. He had made her happy. What an extraordinarily uplifting experience it was to so please another. He was not quite sure if he had ever truly pleased a woman since he had grown to be a man, at least outside of a bedroom. Nor had he ever wanted to, until just this moment.

In the back of her mind she smiled to herself, silently noting that the Blade never once stepped on her toes, and in fact made her feel graceful and light. It was with a small tug of resistance that she left his side and took the arm of a Mr. Peter Willows for the next dance.

Her eyes were still glowing when her mother saw her over the breakfast table.

"Whatever time did all of you arrive home last night?" Cornelia asked as she buttered her scone. "I fear I thought the clock was striking five in the morning when you were all making such a commotion coming in."

Since neither Randolph nor Lydia had yet made it to the table, it was left to Mary to explain that it had indeed been as late as that. "Mama, you must not scold, for I vow I had the loveliest evening. I danced every dance. And I had two escorts—one that took me in to the supper, and yet another who took me in to the midnight repast."

Her mother's scone halted halfway to her mouth, and she had first rounded and then narrowed eyes as she stared at her daughter. "Truly?" she asked somewhat unsteadily.

"Truly. Oh, Mama, there is another ball only one week hence, and I can hardly wait to attend! What should I wear, do you think?"

Cornelia nodded her head at the proper moments, and once or twice murmured "mm-hmm", but otherwise it was Mary who went on for twenty minutes as her mother looked upon her with suddenly hopeful and expectant eyes. Could her maiden daughter finally be attracting the opposite gender? Were the girl's marital hopes rising from the ashes of spinsterhood? From the positive bloom in her daughter's face, Cornelia felt a growing belief in the miracle.

The Duke handed her up into the carriage, where she settled beside Mrs. Hummold. He crawled in after her, apologizing for the rain he brought in with him, and settled next to Mr. Bretwyn.

"I understand that we are to have an interior picnic," Mary said to the attractive man across from her. His hair was wavy, and lightly touched with silver at the temples. He was very distinguished in appearance, despite the smile lines that ran from his nose to his mouth, or perhaps because of them.

"Quite right. I suggested it to the old man there. Said 'Why not a picnic at my Sussex place?' We can't let the rain run our lives forever, and it's really not all that far out, and we can chat a bit as we toodle our way along."

"How delightful."

"Lady Wagnall, I wonder if you knew that we have met before our introductions at the Frelorns's cotillion?" Lettice Hummold asked.

"Oh, I am sorry. I regret to say I don't recall—"

"Nor should you, for we were all in masks," Lettice explained with a friendly smile. "I was the Fancy Bird that helped you when your headpiece broke at the masquerade that Lord and Lady Upton held last fall."

"Oh, how marvelous that we should meet again then, for I never had the chance to thank you," Mary cried.

"Well, as I recall, you did me the favor of setting my headpiece to rights, so I always considered that thanks enough."

"I wondered for weeks afterward who you might have been under those feathers."

"And how were you dressed, Lady Wagnall? Perhaps you and I had occasion to speak as well, without knowing. I came as a pirate. Even borrowed my brother's saber, he being a navy man and all," Charles spoke up.

"I was dressed as a princess of old. My mask was

attached to the conical hat I wore. The hat was too heavy, and I had to walk about with one hand holding it up in place, until eventually the mask tore away from it. That is when Mrs. Hummold assisted me in removing it."

"Ah, so then we did not speak. But I do recall that I wondered if supporting one's hat was an actual affectation from the days of the knights," Charles said, and his expression was so reflective of his bemusement at the time, that Mary had to smile at him.

The ride passed in gay conversation, making the journey seem short. Godfrey was in an excellent mood, and Mary found herself thinking that his was still the sleek, observant demeanor of a tiger, only at the moment the tiger was at play. He was obviously relaxed with these two that had joined them, and there was no need for him to be anything but pleasantly diverted.

When they arrived at their destination, he leaped from the carriage first, assisting the ladies and jovially stating that Charles could carry the picnic basket as he himself was quite occupied with a lady for each arm. He led them quickly through the rain, through the door that had been opened at the sound of carriage wheels, and past a beaming housekeeper. Charles struggled in behind them, mumbling good-naturedly about overstuffed baskets meant to feed a hundred rather than four.

The ride had been of some length, so they set about laying out their repast at once, with the housekeeper, Mrs. Briggins, being sent upon a number of tasks, including a need for glassware, utensils, and warm, wet towels to cleanse one's hands before eating.

They sat on the floor, which was covered by a thin

blue square of bedclothes, and the ladies served, passing high-piled plates to the gentlemen, after which they served themselves. A footman hovered nearby with an ever-ready bottle of wine, and the meal was filled with laughter and light conversation. When Mrs. Briggins brought forth a fresh-baked apricot tart, they all groaned, for they were already replete, but yet the sweet was temptingly aromatic. The Duke talked them all into trying 'just a slice' and commenced to serve up half the tart in gargantuan proportions, gaining Mrs. Briggins admiration for all eternity as he rolled his eyes and smacked his lips and cleared his plate.

"Here, you must eat what is left of mine," Mary said with mock harshness, thrusting the plate in his direction as punishment for the immensity of the slice.

He accepted the plate, pretended to be overwhelmed, and slowly fell over backwards so that he was stretched out upon the ground, except for the plate which was still held safely aloft. Mary was at first astonished to see The Blade allowing himself to play the dunce, but then she could only join the others as they all roared with laughter, and even Mrs. Briggins cried out, "I tarted him to death!", which only gained more laughter, so that mirthful tears actually rolled down Mary's face.

As they sat about, Mary dabbing at her eyes and grinning spasmodically, they fell back into conversation, which turned to the running of Mr. Bretwyn's estate, which naturally led to a proposal to have a look around.

He led them about the house, and then they climbed back in the carriage to drive about the grounds, for the rain was falling steadily, as ever, and they could not stroll about. He pointed out his hydration system, which was a series of water control gates built into the stream that wandered through his lands, and he and the Duke fell into a serious discussion of animal and pest control.

"Really?" asked Charles. "I've never heard of it. They're called O'Brien's snares, did you say?"

"My steward assures me we have never before caught so many rabbits as this past season. I plan to invest in a few more, as the beasts have all but destroyed the kitchen gardens in recent years. We've had to purchase a deal of our produce, and that's expensive business."

"Oh, terribly, terribly," Charles agreed as the carriage came to a halt. "Well, that's the whole of it, then, ladies. I hope the Duke and I were not too tiresome, but we landowners must be vigilant in the maintenance of the home farm."

"Quite the thing," Mrs. Hummold said approvingly. She turned to Mary and went on, "Charles is very clever in his investments, and takes good care of his tenants. I have always said he would go far, if he had the right person beside him."

Mary cast a quick glance toward Godfrey, who looked down with approval upon the lady's head.

"Every man should have a wife to help him in this life," Godfrey said, not even smiling a little at his hypocritical statement.

"Exactly so," Mrs. Hummold beamed upon the Duke.

"All one had to do was look to see that the houses and grounds are well taken care of," Mary said, a little flustered.

Mrs. Hummold realized at once that she had set her own mind open to viewing, for it became a suddenly obvious and a nearly tangible thing in the air between them, that she thought it was time for her brother to take a wife, and that she had decided this day that Mary would do quite nicely in the position.

Mary blushed red to the roots of her hair, for the lady had given what was tantamount to her approval. Even as she blushed, she reminded herself that the Duke had said he would help her find a husband, not that it would be a matter for delicacy and discretion in the pursuit thereof. That she had so soon gained this mark of favor ought to be a good sign, but Mary could not hide the confusion that filled her.

Mrs. Hummold saw the effects of her words upon the younger woman, and her own eyes filled with distress. "My dear," she said. "I . . . I . . . would you care for tea?" she flustered.

For a moment Mary could not raise her head, but then the thought came to her: *children, children, children,* and she forced her chin up. She looked first to the Duke, who finally had the grace to look a little uncomfortable, then to Charles, who had evidently missed any innuendos, and finally to Mrs. Hummold.

"Oh," that lady said faintly, seeing the newborn determined, almost angry gleam in Mary's eye, one which immediately softened as the younger woman said, "Yes, I would dearly care for a cup of tea."

Mrs. Hummold sat frozen a moment longer, then a tremulous smile came to her lips, in which she accepted that her gaffe had been forgiven.

Charles looked from one to the other, a faint, puzzled frown between his brows until Godfrey clapped him on the back and pointed out the carriage door, stating, "Lead on, my good fellow. And do let us have these bricks reheated before we start off to London, eh what?"

The tea was very pleasant, with not a soul touching the tiny, lovely cakes on the tray, but for Mary a little of the magic of the day had left. 'Business' had transpired over the top of her pleasure. She was out and about, with the Duke, for the soul purpose of finding a husband, and she must not forget it.

The ride back to London was not so giddy as before, and in fact after Charles had yawned for the third time, they took Godfrey's advice and all settled back on the squabs, dropping off into a doze one by one.

They awoke as the carriage jolted to a halt, and laughed a little with one another, faintly embarrassed to be caught out dozing despite their mutual assent earlier. When the tiger had opened the carriage door, Charles made as though to descend to assist Mary out of the carriage, but Godfrey stuck out a foot, barring the way. "Allow me," he murmured, only moving his foot out of the way when Charles retreated to his seat.

As he took her hand and steadied her upon the ground, his mouth came close enough to her ear to murmur, "Tough business, this."

It was enough; he need say no more, for she was entirely weak toward him. He could dispel her megrims with but a few words. "Thank you for a lovely day," she said with a gentle nod.

The rallying of her spirits was rewarded by a light coming into his features. An impish grin flickered into being, and he asked in a very low voice, "Care to bag this one, madam?"

"He's very nice," she said noncommittally.

"Clever girl. Keep your options open. There's more on a level with this one."

"Whatever are you two doing, standing about whispering in the rain?" Mrs. Hummold called from the carriage's interior.

"Tuesday, at three," he said then, by way of a parting as he climbed back into the vehicle.

There was only enough time for her to nod her agreement to this sudden pronouncement of future plans, having no idea what it was beyond the day and time.

Her family asked after the excursion over dinner, and she rambled on a bit about the meal and the estate. Her mother nodded at the pleasantness of the day her daughter had spent, her father said he was glad there was a solid fellow such as Mr. Bretwyn along, elsewise he would think twice before letting his daughter go about with such a rackety one as Lord Rothayne, and Lydia changed the conversation entirely to a discussion of whether she and her daughters ought to have matching dresses made for the annual derby days coming in August.

It was only Mrs. Pennett who saw shadows behind the smile in her charge's eyes, but try as she might, she could only solicit comments about how pleasant a day it had been.

As she tucked herself into bed that night, Mary contemplated the prying inquiries Gladys had made. How did one explain the ache that came from having someone do for you exactly what you asked them to, and not what you really wanted? How did you say aloud that a bit of your heart was bruised because you were imperfect and could not have the fairytale ending? No, it was all silliness, and it served her right that she felt all befuddled in her mind, for she kept forgetting that a ring on her finger was the purpose behind her gay life these days. *Enjoy the wine, but do not allow yourself to become drunk upon it,* she chided herself as she slid toward slumber.

Mary had her outing with Lord Revenshaven, who took her to see the opera. He was very pleasant, and knew quite a bit about the music. Mary enjoyed his comments, for she was somewhat musically inclined herself, and found it entertaining to discuss the various arias and chorus ensembles they had witnessed. They enjoyed sips of champagne and some of the dainties that the theatre offered for sale. Afterward, when Mrs. Pennett escorted her charge back into the house, that lady prattled on a bit about the gracious manners of the Lord Revenshaven, all comments with which Mary could not disagree. She was not sure she had made much of an impression herself, however, for Lord Revenshaven had not asked if he might see her again, or if he might come to call. Mary could not be unduly disturbed, however, for tomorrow evening she was to go with Lt. Hargood to a dinner play. It might sting to have a gentleman be lukewarm to one's company, but it was the briefest sting when one considered that another gent had requested the favor for the very next day.

The play was a farce, entitled, "The Cousin's Sister's Husband's Wife," and it was a little risqué. At first Mary did not know if she ought to laugh at the crudities and the innuendos, for Lt. Hargood's face was stoically arranged. After pretending to cough several times into her napkin, she accidentally caught the lieutenant's eye, and then they were laughing together. They then gave themselves up to an evening of mild vulgarity, and enjoyed themselves very well.

Mrs. Pennett pretended to disapprove, for a while anyway, until Mary caught her grinning at a lewd joke.

After it was over, he apologized, even while he laughed a little. "I had no idea! I suppose the title should have tipped me off, but . . .!"

"I will not think that you are wicked if you will not think it of me," Mary smiled.

"I never could. No, it takes a true lady to make a bloke feel comfortable in such a situation."

"Why, I thank you for the compliment, Lieutenant."

"But it *was* funny when the husband walked in on them, wasn't it?" And then they were laughing again.

They laughed and talked for another hour, until finally the proprietor discreetly requested that they leave, that he might close his establishment.

Mary was greatly pleased when, as he left her at her front door, Lt. Hargood asked if he might come to call soon. "Of course," had been her answer.

When she went inside she looked through the bits of correspondence the butler had set aside for each member of the family. She found several invitations to parties in her pile, and among them was a note from the Duke. She broke the seal and read the contents, which merely read:

You're not here! I will assume you will receive me tomorrow morning. At ten. Until then—
Your Adoring,
Godfrey

Of course she would receive him. Even if she had had plans, she would have cancelled them, for Godfrey was coming tomorrow.

* * *

Mary was dressed and waiting in the front parlor by 9:45. She was plying her needle absentmindedly while actually glancing out of the corner of her eye toward the view of the drive. What did the Blade have in mind today? Was Mr. Bretwyn to be a part of this excursion? When she saw the carriage arrive, she glanced even more surreptitiously, intrigued to see two strangers come from the vehicle after Godfrey.

She waited, almost patiently, until her visitors were announced, and put the embroidery hoop aside as they were led into the room. She smoothed her gown—one of her prettiest ones—and when the butler had bowed himself out, made them a pretty curtsy.

"Mary, you look lovely today," the Duke said, smiling as he took her hands. He turned at once to the couple that had followed him into the room. "Lord and Lady Faver, this is Lady Wagnall. Mary, please meet Lord Thomas Faver, and his aunt, Lady Evelyn Faver."

They murmured their how-do-you-dos, and then Godfrey announced, "We are off to the British Museum today."

It was not as jolly a carriage party as the one with Charles Bretwyn had been, for the Lord and the Lady Faver were not of the kind to be silly, but they were very pleasant, and Mary and Lady Faver discovered they had read many books in common.

"For myself, I do not care what her detractors say of Mrs. Ratcliffe. And even though there are whispers that 'she' is really a 'he,' I have enjoyed every book so far written under that *nom de plume*."

Mary nodded, saying, "The books are filled with excitement, one cannot deny that."

61

Seeing that the gentlemen were looking skeptical at their announcements, Lady Favor changed topics by inquiring, "Do you go to Lord Malter's this evening?"

"Oh, yes, I am so looking forward to it. I understand that Maestro D'Allicio will be performing for us. I have heard he is most remarkable in his talent," Mary said enthusiastically.

"I have had the pleasure of hearing Maestro D'Allicio sing before, and it is true, he is a marvel."

"Mary sings beautifully herself, and has quite the ear for pitch and style. I will be interested in soliciting her opinion after the performance," Godfrey said.

"Do you indeed, Lady Wagnall?" Lord Faver inquired. He was one of the youngest that had stood up with her, his face free of any lines as yet, and his cravat as high as was currently fashionable even though he did not quite have the length of neck to support such a structure, and so must pivot his head most carefully, if at all. He did, however, have dark, inquisitive eyes, a reflection of a learned and eager mind, and he was every inch a gentleman. Mary had begun to like him right away, despite the fact that he was perhaps a bit shy of speaking up in the company of ladies.

The museum was not crowded, so they could admire the displays at their leisure. Lord Faver proved to be something of an authority on Renaissance sculpture, and the Duke entertained them all with true tales of the lives of the artists.

Afterward they treated themselves to ices at Gunther's. As they proceeded to return to the Favers' home, they agreed to look for one another at tonight's festivity.

"I shall ask after this rascal here," Lady Faver said warningly toward Mary, but with an eye on Godfrey. "I cannot like leaving you unescorted in a closed vehicle together, but since it is only three blocks to Wagnall Hall from here, I shall pretend it is acceptable."

"My lady, she is safe as a babe with me," the Duke replied, but all sincerity was negated by the smile that went with the statement.

"Cad!" Lady Faver trilled, striking him on the sleeve with her unopened fan. "Look for us at the ball. We'll be there, though 'tis bound to be another crush, I daresay. Lord Malter does not, in my opinion, believe in moderation," Lady Faver added somewhat tartly.

"You will save a dance for me, won't you, Lady Wagnall?" Lord Faver asked as he leaned toward Mary just prior to climbing down. He flushed a little at his own presumption.

"Of course, the first waltz," Mary replied.

"Until then," the fellow replied, and for a moment she thought he might take up her hand and kiss the back of it, but he did not.

As the carriage pulled away, Godfrey leaned forward and gathered her hands into his own. True to his word, he had shown little restraint about touching her. If she touched his arm, he took it as a signal that he was free to do the same. If she reached to remove a smudge from his cheek, he then saw nothing wrong with running a finger over her own cheek, smudge or no. If her foot bumped against his boot, he saw no reason not to play silly foot dueling games with her. Now he looked at her earnestly, for all the world unaware that his fingers were massaging her hands and making them tingle, and said,

"Things are going well, wouldn't you say?"

"Yes, I would."

"This Faver fellow — he's a puppy, of course, but you could whip him into shape, I've no doubt. His aunt is not convinced, I think — for I would hazard a guess that you are in her mind possibly a 'conniving older female' — but she has a soft spot for the boy. He's her heir, you see. I think she could be brought around, for his sake, to any plans we would care to make for him." Mere weeks ago he never would have guessed that he would allow so much of his time to be spent in the company of one woman, and yet here he was, leaning forward eagerly to hear her comments. For the first time in a long time he recalled why a person could wish to do good: there was satisfaction to be had from watching Mary blossom under his custody.

"After all this time with the elder gentlemen, I must confess that he does seem a positive infant," she said, one corner of her mouth lifting. "But he is all that is kind and good, it must be said."

"How did your evening with Hargood go? Did Mrs. Pennett care for him?" he inquired.

"Mrs. Pennett? Do you and she discuss me behind my back?"

"Not a bit of it. We discuss you to your face, but that face is often so far gone into the clouds, you take no notice of us."

"That is not true," she sniffed, wondering if, and hoping, it was not. She knew such was his effect on her. She retreated into petulance. "Yes, I am enjoying myself, but is that wrongheaded of me?"

He shook his head once, quickly, and placed one hand upon his chest dramatically. "You ask this of one who is dedicated to enjoying himself? More the fool, you. But you did not answer my question: what of this Lt. Hargood?"

But Mary had turned introspective. "Should I know yet?"

Her sudden question surprised him. "Pardon me?"

"Should I know yet whom it is I should be drawn to? Or is that the best way to go on? Do I target one fellow over another, or wait around to see who comes up to scratch?" A note of bitterness had crept into her voice despite her efforts to repress it.

"A little of both, I should think. If there is one fellow you care for over another, then of course we must plan a line of attack directly upon him. But as it stands now, I think it might be best to allow yourself to go on being seen as available and popular."

"Popular?" she rolled the word around in her mouth. "Am I? Popular?"

"Oh yes, I would say so. You see, my dear, those fellows who have not fallen immediately into parson's trap realize real value a little better than do the callow youths. We . . . they are less likely to think a pretty face always makes a pretty companion. So, now that you have become a 'visual commodity', yes, I should have to say you are a popular one. Oh, not with the widows and the spinsters who have no notion of how to compete, but certainly with the gents."

A glow started in Mary's toes and traveled all the way up to the top of her head, forcing a bright smile onto her face. "How extraordinary!" she cried, and then, "Oh, Godfrey, you cannot know how many times I have thanked heaven that we two should have met."

At that he, too, smiled, but the smile faded after a

short while, and he was almost happy to see that they had arrived at her home. And worst and strangest of all, he was not at all sure why he felt that way.

Chapter Five

Mary was tired. She had been to almost every ball, rout, musical evening, concert, card party, and festivity that had rendered an invitation to the Wagnall household for the past two weeks. Tonight she was supposed to venture out to Lady Salride's affair—it had something to do with an evening of invocations, dances, and other worldly celebrations that supposedly had to do with stopping the fall of rain—but she had finally pled exhaustion and opted to stay home.

She had just settled before the fire, curled up with house slippers on her feet, a shawl across her shoulders, and a thick tome in her hands when a visitor was announced.

"His grace, the Duke of Rothayne," Pendleton heralded, stepping aside to allow the gentleman to enter once he saw his mistress's eager nod of approval.

"Godfrey!" Mary said warmly, starting to rise.

"Pray do not bother," he motioned her to retain her seat.

"I thought you were at Salride's tonight," she said, setting her book aside and waving him to a chair.

"No, I had planned to be, but then when you declined my company, that so put me in the mopes that I actually went home and discovered I had some correspondence awaiting my perusal," he said, settling in the chair opposite hers. He stretched out his long legs and shifted until he was comfortable. She watched him, as always, enjoying the poetry of his motion.

"Is it this self-said correspondence that brings you here tonight?"

"Exactly so. I came to tell you that I have been summoned to the home estate. It seems this blasted rain has all but destroyed our crops this year. My steward is frantic, so you see, I must go."

"Of course you must," she said at once. "I hope I never made you feel beholden—"

"Such talk!" he cried, holding up a hand to cut her off. " 'Tis fustian, between us two. You know I only do what I want."

"So, you *want* to go to the country?"

He laughed then. "All right, perhaps not *always* exactly what I want to do, but, yes, in a way I should like to go and see for myself. It's good land, I warrant, and I hate to see damage done to it. Flooding. Wash-outs. Bad business, I'm afraid. And so I must go, want or no."

"It was good of you to come and tell me," she said sincerely.

"I did not want you to have to receive the news in a note." His expression turned somber, and he examined the bottom-most button on his waistcoat as he went on, "I admit I am leaving my lamb among the wolves, and am not best pleased with doing so. I suppose I came to warn you to be careful while I'm gone. Don't accept anyone's suit too easily. We want you to find and have the best, you know."

She smiled softly at the top of his head, pleasure unfurling in her chest and spreading to all her limbs. For whatever reasons he had, it was true that he had an affection for her. And hers for him was as a light in the darkness. "I promise I shall accept no one while you are gone."

He looked up from the perusal of his button then, and cautioned, "It may be weeks."

She smiled, to let him know she was teasing, and said primly, "Well, *weeks*. I don't know about that, then."

"Imp!" he cried with an impish grin of his own. "For that you must pay a price. I demand a brandy and an hour of your time. I shall need to carry your sweet voice and clever repartee about in my head to sustain me while I am at home." He then actually shuddered.

She raised her eyebrows, a little surprised by the obvious reluctance to return home. It was so unlike him to do what he would rather not, and she could not think it was the flooding that disturbed his peace of mind so.

"Have they no conversation in Kent, Godfrey?" she inquired even as she rose to cross the room and pour his brandy.

"Too much, my love. *That* is the problem: there is far too much conversation."

"You were never one to avoid the gay life," she said, returning and handing him a snifter.

" 'Tis never gay. You see, my heart, I have a deep dark secret, a miserable secret that is forever threatening to overtake me."

She knew that now he spoke lightly, so she was not adverse to asking what he meant. "Deep and dark, you say? You must tell me."

"Sisters," he replied heavily. "I have eight sisters."

"Truly?" she cried. It was well known that the Rothayne clan was a large one, but such was the man's presence that she had never thought to question him on his home life.

"And, worse yet, I am 'the baby'. And the only son. The beloved heir. I tell you, it is a heinous title, a terrible weight."

She laughed, "But surely they love you?"

"They love me too well. All eight of them. Father is safe and tidy in his grave, and so you see that if you include Mother, then I am surrounded by nine females, with nary a male in sight," he groaned. He shook his head, his eyes filled with a horror that was perhaps not all pretense, and he sipped at his brandy in a brooding manner.

"You poor soul," she murmured, unable to keep from grinning at his discomfort.

"I am that. Could I have not had a brother or two? Could I not have been born first? No, I tell you, fate loves me not. She placed me in the most awkward position."

"But surely most of your sisters are in London during the season?" She made a half-attempt to comfort him, covering her grin by raising a hand to shield her mouth.

"They've all gone to the country. It is time for Georgette's lying-in, you see. It is sure to be an hysterical event. My mother hopes for a grandson, as she already has fourteen granddaughters." He sat up abruptly. "Oh, sweet merciful heavens! I did not even consider that most of my nieces will be there as well! I shall be surrounded!"

"I wonder at *our* relationship," Mary said mildly, returning to her chair and arranging the shawl more satisfactorily about her shoulders. "I am, in case you failed to note, a female. I should think that would put me quite out of favor in your eyes."

"But you're not my demmed sister, or my mother. And I must not be the slightest bit proper with you, as I have just proven by the language I have chosen to use

70

in your presence. *That* makes all the difference, I assure you."

"So you think of me as, let us say, being one of the 'fellows'?" she asked, a trifle archly, frowning just a little bit.

He raised the snifter to his lips, slumping even further into the chair's recesses. His face lost its honesty, and returned to its more normal state of amusement. "Oh, hardly that, Mary. I've never wondered what it would be like to lay down with Mr. Bretwyn, or any of the other 'fellows', but I assure you I have wondered the same about you."

Her breath caught in her lungs, but she forcibly ignored her own body's traitorous reaction. She fought to smoothly recover her breathing, to make the blood begin pulsing through her veins again, but not to race to her face. She cast about in her mind for something to say, having entirely lost the ability to converse under the weight of his caressing gaze. "So your family wishes you to produce an heir?" she said, and had to fight once again to keep from blushing at the inappropriately timed remark.

"They believe I am their only hope for another male. Silly, but it is what they believe."

Her ears were ringing, and her palms were moist, and she felt the biggest fool. He was teasing, of course, just as usual, but his intimate comment had surprised her, caught her offguard. She had not had time to steel herself against him. Or perhaps it was merely a natural response of being alone, unchaperoned, with him . . . or any man, she told herself fiercely.

He was looking at her, and she was supposed to be saying something, and so words fell out of her mouth haphazardly. "Have you then no offspring at all?"

Surprise registered on his face now, and then

he threw back his head and howled with laughter.

After a moment, she giggled with him, for it was an infectious laugh, and she was so flustered and embarrassed and lacking in control over herself that she could only laugh along with him, losing her battle with the blush.

"Ah, Mary, you are a pet! I am glad to see I am at last bringing you about," he said, wiping at his eyes with a handkerchief produced from his coat pocket. "But to answer your question: no, I have none that have claimed me, nor have any females raged at me about such 'expectations'. I admit freely that I discovered early in life that it is wise to make love to women who are married, for they blithely pass the product of their sins on to their husbands."

Still unsettled and half-giddy, she asked flippantly, "Have you no gentler feelings, your grace?"

"Indeed, I do. And now I shall shock you, by telling you that if I knew of any offspring I would not hesitate to provide for them. Ah, I see I have surprised you. But, my dearest Mary, I am but a mere mortal man, and mortal men do love to see themselves recreated, whichever side of the blanket it does occur upon." He raised the snifter to his lips, one leg crossing over the other, his posturing daring her to reproach him.

She had sobered and steadied under his truthful revelations, and it was with something more like her usual clear-headedness that she said, "Yes, you *have* surprised me. But not for the worse. I will tell you, it makes me like you even a little more than before. I did not know you had such a romantic side."

One booted foot began to swing idly as he replied in a sly voice, "Ah, but I can be very romantic. May I demonstrate upon yourself?"

She picked up her book and tossed it at him. He

ducked to one side, and it bounced harmlessly away. "Lust, your grace, is not romance," she admonished.

"Is it not?" he asked in mock ingenuity.

"No."

"Fancy that. Have you told anyone of this observation? It seems to me it is the kind of thing that ought to get about."

"I believe I would be safe in saying that had you attended church but once you might have known this for yourself."

"Oh well, then, you can see why I avoid the place."

He stayed for another half an hour, making her laugh so much that her brother came down to see what all the frivolity was about. Godfrey made his farewells to them both, pledging to write to Mary, and leaving his country address that she might do the same.

"I say, Mary, what were you doing down here all alone with that fellow?" Randolph asked her as soon as the Duke had been escorted out.

"Oh, piffle, Randolph. The man means me no harm whatsoever."

"There's your reputation to see to, Mary. Servants talk, you know."

"Not about old maids," was Mary's acerbic reply.

"Now, Mary, that's no way—"

"Good night, Randolph. I am going to bed." She gave him her back and proceeded upstairs, where she put herself in to bed, desiring no one's company, not even a maid's, and particularly not that of the sharp-eyed Mrs. Pennett.

As usual, she lay reviewing the day, and assessing her part in it. She came quickly, though perhaps not quite easily, to a momentous decision: she knew what she must do. She knew there was a price to be paid for keeping the Duke of Rothayne as her confederate. She knew she could be amused by him; that she could let him show her his views and unstifled opinions; that she could even allow him to warm her heart and tickle her fancy; but she must never, *ever* let him near enough to turn that warmth into fire, for she was as kindling, ready to be consumed rapidly by the merest touch of the flame that he was.

She could either go on as she had, rather like a child playing with a candle — dangerous, an accident waiting to happen — or she could change things around in her mind, let him be just like the light that illuminates the stained glass windows of a cathedral. He was the source of beauty that was forever beyond her reach. There must be glass between the sunlight and the observer — a window, beautiful but unobtainable, that divided them for all the days they were to call themselves friends. There could be, then, no errant touches, no friendly kisses on the cheek, no more time spent alone together. He must remain, forever, just remote enough that she could bask in the glow of his companionship without being rendered to ashes.

As she allowed her body to slide toward slumber, she forced her thoughts through an evaluation of the several gentlemen who had shown a measure of interest in her company, but it was not of them she dreamed when slumber at last overtook her.

Chapter Six

It was exactly two weeks and two and one-half days before Mary's mother announced over the breakfast table, "You've received a letter from the Duke."

Mary looked up with expectant eyes, watching carefully as the letter was passed down the table toward her. It was not uncommon for their extended family to gather from their various homes (which Mary privately thought saw a lot less of them than did herself) on a Saturday morning for a repast together. When Lydia extended her hand to pass on the letter, Mary all but snatched it from her, but then she settled it next to her plate, unopened.

"Aren't you going to read it?" Lydia asked.

"Yes," was Mary's tight-lipped answer.

"Soon?"

"Yes."

Lydia pursed her lips as well, and promptly abandoned her little sister to turn instead and grill her sister-in-law as to what she was going to do today. She'd had years of experience at trying to squeeze blood from that particular turnip, and she was not going to waste another moment on the fruitless effort of trying to get Mary to do something she did not want to do.

Mary ate a few more bites to establish a sense of

propriety, but then she quietly made her excuses, slipped the letter into the pocket of her morning gown, and hurried away upstairs to her room. There, she sliced open the wax seal with her letter opener, and greedily read:

My Sweetest Mary —

How I long for your company! You cannot imagine the daily torture I endure. I am emasculated. I am trampled. I am as nothing more than a source of gleeful vindictiveness to these persons I must call my relations! I, who love the ladies well and often (ah, I can see the glowing red tips of your precious tiny ears even from here, my own) now find I am stranded amongst the coldest and cruelest of all females — my siblings.

My only comfort comes with solitude, for I ride several times daily, when they are willing to accept my pleas that I have duties as a landowner. I find the properties in sad estate, but not quite destitute. I fear it will be a hard year for the poorer of the district, and have therefore ordered my steward to desist from trapping rabbits. Perhaps it is true that I am therefore encouraging unlawful poaching, but I cannot see the harm when people are hungry. The curious side effect of all this rain is that at least the rabbit-beasts have had many green shoots upon which to dine, and so have mostly left the private gardens alone. We shall at least not have to absorb the cost of filling the pantry this season.

Georgette is still not delivered of her first child. I rather pointedly told her to do so last night, but it seems she ignored me. I am hopeful that the poor, dear child that comes of this blessed event will draw, at least for a while, some attention from myself. (I can hear you saying "What a conceit'!" and of course that is quite true.)

Remember to keep the gents at arm's length . . .

well, perhaps a little closer, for we do wish that you shall marry fairly soon. But beware of the 'nice ones', for they usually are not truly so in many ways, I've found. I hope and pray that I shall be returning to London soon. (You see, then, your influence on me — I am now praying.)

> *Your mostly obedient and completely*
> *affectionate friend,*
> *Godfrey.*

She read it again twice, smiling all the while, feeling almost as though he were there in the room with her, for his written word was just as his spoken word. She nodded over the wisdom of letting the rabbits find their way into someone's stew pot, and she found herself putting up a tiny prayer that Godfrey should find himself blessed with a new *nephew* soon.

That night when she dressed for the musical evening at Madam Windom-Holly's, during which she had agreed to play the harp as accompaniment to Miss Antonia Windom-Holly, it was not of the music that she thought, but of Godfrey's letter. She had known, of course, that she was going to miss his company. Her life was no less active and merry with his absence, for she was now firmly established in her growing circle of acquaintances, but the special thrill of hearing him sum up any situation quickly and piercingly was lacking. No one else dared to say quite exactly what they thought, or even if they did they did so clumsily and sometimes even cruelly, whereas she had learned that Godfrey saved his stings only for himself or those who had a talent for unkindnesses. When Mr. Hann might elbow her and indicate the ridiculously bright waistcoat of a contemporary, Godfrey would say how glad he was that someone was not afraid of a little color. If Miss Hennings commented on another girl's lack of grace, Godfrey would, without fail, be the next to stand up with the girl. That he also was a fine enough dancer to help the poor creature look a little more to advantage was to his credit also.

Yes, his was a curiously honest nature, not bound by conventional rules, and he was therefore also not always well liked. He made more than one fellow angry when he refused to drink or play cards with the chap, but, as he privately told Mary, he was not about to fleece a half-drunk man-child out of his inheritance, nor watch as he made a fool of himself. Some ladies adored him, for his clever tongue was also sincere with its compliments, but then others could not see the intellect and the humor behind the risqué comments he must forever issue. He shocked and he thrilled, and it was exciting to know him, to be in any degree close to him. That he should write to her was but another sign of his regard . . . and it caused her to sigh now at his absence even though she knew the evening ahead promised to be a pleasant one.

Even though she returned home late, she sat down at once and wrote in return:

Dearest Godfrey,
How shall I say my evening went tonight? I played the harp for Miss Antonia Windom-Holly, and though normally she has a fine voice, tonight it was quite unsteady. I believe I know the reason why, and I believe that reason is called Lord Trumble. He is very young, perhaps twenty, and flushed of face, but with lovely brown curls, over-long, which I must say rather suits him. She spent the entire evening glancing at him and then away, and every time she did so, her sweet little voice quite lost its nerve. It must be said that Lord Trumble did not seem to notice the lack. I believe we shall have news in that quarter soon.
Even as I sit here writing I wonder if your sister has

brought another of the Rothayne clan among us. Is it a fifteenth granddaughter? Oh, surely not! It boggles the mind.

Tonight Mr. Bretwyn asked me to accompany him, his sister, and her husband, William Hummold, to Vauxhall Gardens. Now I know that for a young girl this would be considered most inappropriate, but since I am not that, and since we are just going for the fireworks, and since Mrs. Hummold has not caviled, neither shall I.

A new gentleman has come upon my horizons. His name is Lord Spafford. He is very dark of skin, due he says to his devotion to time spent aboard his ships. (Yes, I said the plural: ships). He races them, and apparently wins quite often, with himself at the helm. He has a large laugh—almost frightening until one becomes accustomed to the sound—and is very knowledgeable. We have found ourselves moving to the side of a dance floor and spending many minutes talking. (Do not fear, Mrs. Pennett sees that I do not become monopolized.)

Lt. Hargood, alas, has been called back to active duty. I did not get his address—such as a soldier's may be—but he has mine and vows he will write. He left for foreign soils over a week ago. Pity, he was the best dancer I've met, besides yourself.

Come home soon, dear friend. London is stifling without you.

> *Your very weary (it is four in*
> *the morning) and yawning friend,*
> *Mary.*

She went to Vauxhall Gardens with Mr. Bretwyn and Mrs. Hummold, where she was bid to please call them 'Charles' and 'Letitia'. She graciously accepted the tribute, and of course extended the same permission to them, secretly storing up the fact for her next letter to Godfrey.

His next letter came a week later, and this time her brother and sister were breakfasting in their own homes, Mother was still abed, and Father was already gone from the house. Mary read her letter at table, laughing out loud once, unexpectedly, spraying coffee across the tablecloth. She coughed and held a hand to her breast and tried to breath, swallow, and giggle all at once.

Beloved Mary—

I have sat down at once, upon receiving your letter. It was as manna from heaven! There is still society out there! There is still peace, and tranquility! How I long for the early morning rumble of market carts beneath my window. How I long for the filthy oaths that the hawkers fling at one another at indecently early hours. Where is the ragged cough, the scrape and clatter of the lamplighter's ladder as he makes his rounds, snuffing out the gas lamps he set flaring the night before? I tell you, these sounds, so annoying to the average countryman, would be as a lullaby to me! I know what it is to reside in the dark reaches of hell, for hell is seated here, in Kent. I tell you, at last I understand why the preachers bid us all be good and not wicked, for this place I name hell is a place beyond hope, a place we should all strive mightily to avoid!

There is happy news that is laced with sorrow: Georgette was safely delivered of a healthy, pink and lustily wailing child— another girl, of course. My mother was heard to cry that it defies the laws of nature to have yet another female born to us, but whatever else she may have said, I missed, for I was weeping into my cravat. (Though, truth be told, I am not sure I am quite wicked enough to wish that a poor

*boy-child should have to be raised in such a bevy of fe-
males as was I — nay, even more of them than I had. It
seems a cruelty. Perhaps Nature knows this, and therefore gave unto us Baby Jessica, to spare any poor lad
such a fate.)*

*Work is progressing on the farmlands. We had to
dig a new pond, to which we have drained several
fields. I never knew these fields to flood when I was
younger, and so that tells you how extraordinary the
amount of rain we have had truly is. It has been better
of late here — I have hopes that some year the rain will
stop entirely. My steward was all but ill unto death
when he saw the prime land we had to give over to
making the pond, but nothing is truly 'prime' under
water, now is it? and so I told him. It is clear we shall
have to rebuild the stone fence about the north edge of
the property. Its footings were all but washed away
from under it, so it is broken and uneven and almost
beyond repairing. We may have to tear it down entirely, and start anew.*

*The crops are dead and rotting. I have some land in
southern Scotland that I have been assured will produce some income this year, but it is painful to bring
the profits from one merely to repair the lost ones of
the other. Nothing for it though. At least there has not
been disease (I shall now knock on some wood) in
either the animals nor the people.*

*You would not believe what my sisters have been
doing to me lately . . . No, I cannot say. It is too grue-
some.*

*Please write to me again. I admit I thoroughly en-
joyed envisioning you there at four in the morning,
dressed in naught but a flimsy nightrail, your long,
lovely chestnut hair loose about your shoulders, that
frown of concentration across your forehead, your
sweet lips pursed in thought. To think of such a vision*

*was as a balmy breeze, a cool draft sent to me, your
captive friend in Hades.*

> *With hopes of a homecoming soon,*
> *Godfrey.*

She sat blushing over her plate, for he was not here and could not chide her for the crimson in her cheeks. A little flash of something that threatened to take away her breath came into her head, but it was firmly and rigidly pushed outside the scope of her interior vision. It was his way to make every situation into a provocative one, and she would only be a fool to do anything but laugh along with him, even in absentia.

When she went up to her room, she burned the letter. She told herself she did it so that no one would ever come across it and misinterpret the harmless jests he made, but in truth she did so because she was silently afraid that she might be the one to do so.

Mary turned to see that the Baronet Stephens was coming her way. She immediately turned on her heel and slipped between two couples, heading randomly in any direction opposite his own. Lord Stephens was not a man to be denied, however, for within fifteen minutes she found herself cornered.

"Lady Wagnall, how pleasant to see you tonight. I was hoping to put my name to your program," he said, a trifle breathlessly.

She gave him a cool smile before she murmured, "Of course."

"Your program . . .?" he prompted when she did not extend the card at once.

Reluctantly she handed it to him.

"Ah, I see the next dance is free! How fortunate. It shall be mine then. And this one, after the midnight repast, too—"

"I do not dance twice, my lord," she interrupted him.

"No, no, of course not," he hastened to say, but there was a slight frown hovering about his mouth.

"Unless I have known someone a great time," she amended, for she knew as well as he that she had given more than one dance to a number of gentlemen. It was just, simply, that she did not care for Lord Stephens. He was often overbearing, with a pushiness that he only sometimes bothered to cloak in seemliness. Next to Godfrey's freshness, Lord Stephens suffered. He was the epitome of all that was stuffy yet imprudent, pompous yet lowering in their society. And even though it was quite true that he was very plump of pocket, Mary knew for a certainty that this was one field from which she did not care to reap.

She liked him so little, in fact, that when the music began for the next set she tried to remain hidden behind the punch bowl and its attendant fronds and flowers, but his eye was too sharp for that. As he claimed her hand, she pretended to have forgotten. Just as the set was forming, she sent up a little prayer of gratitude that it was to be a country dance and not a waltz.

He had his dance, and though his fingers gripped too tightly, and his body swayed too near her own during the movements, and his habit of staring without saying a word was once again exhibited, it could have been worse. She thought to herself gratefully that at least now she could go on with the evening without having to try and avoid his company, for he knew he could not solicit another dance from her this day.

But she was mistaken, for though the dance was ended, she could not leave the man behind. He followed her from group to group, ignored Mrs. Pennett's not-so-subtle requests for punch or tea or a slice of cake, and stood awaiting Mary's exodus from the floor when she had gone off to dance with other fellows that he might rejoin her. More than once she exited the dance in the exact opposite direction of where he stood waiting, but every time he worked his way back to her side, and joined in her conversations whether she would have him there or no.

Finally, in exasperation she excused herself to her hostess, and to the gentlemen who still had their dances unclaimed upon her program, and left early. Mrs. Pennett frowned all the way home, though they were both so wearied by the Lord Stephens that by mutual consent they did not even speak of what a nuisance he had made of himself.

Mary's spirits lifted immediately upon her return home, however, for there was another letter from Godfrey. It read:

My heart,

I am a weak man. I admit it. I have therefore crumbled under the weight of my imprisonment here, and though it is the height of the season, and though it is all that is selfish and unthinking in myself, I am writing to plead with you that you should come and rescue me. That's right, sweet Mary, I need you here, to give me comfort, to rest mine weary head upon thy lap, to have thee as a shield before me — staving off my sisters with a stick if necessary. They will not heed me. They will not give me a moment's peace. But you! Mary, they will listen to you, for you would be their guest, and they have that much in manners anyway. Or so I dare to hope.

Say you will come. For a week. For a day. Even an hour. It will save my sanity, I vow it!

To show my good faith, I will even say that you are to bring your chaperone, Mrs. Pennett. She is a fine

and sensible lady, to whom you could pass that stav-
ing stick once in a while, that we might have some re-
lief from the Dragons of Kent. Yea, even bring your
mother! Your father. Your siblings! I shall feed them
all, and gladly, for the sake of seeing you once again
before I am driven mad.

Come at once. Do not reply. Come. As you love me,
you will come. At once. Please. I beg of you, please,
come!

Godfrey.

She read the letter again, holding it in one hand as
she smiled to herself, and even as she reached to drag
out the old traveling case from under the bed with the
other.

Chapter Seven

"Mary!" Godfrey called jubilantly, his deep voice carrying. His enthusiasm was so great upon seeing her carriage upon his drive that she was treated to the rare occasion of seeing the Duke actually run. His grin was wide as he sprinted by twos down the stone steps of his front entrance, his hatless hair ruffled by the wind and burnished to copper by the dim light of the gray day. She waited, pulling back her foot from the step the ostler had just lowered, as Godfrey came up to the carriage in a rush, grabbing either side of the doorframe and thrusting his head and shoulders within. "Mary!" he said again, but this time it was more a purr than a shout.

She could only gasp when he reached in, placed his large and manicured hands around her waist, and physically drew her out. Before her feet could touch the ground, he had caught her up in a bear hug and was spinning her around, laughing. "My angel of mercy! It is true: heaven does indeed answer our prayers, for you are *here!*"

"Godfrey!" she laughed breathlessly as he finally set her on her feet. Mrs. Pennett came from the carriage, her surprise at the greeting reflected only in the minute lifting of her eyebrows.

"How many bags did you bring?" he asked, eyeing the top of the carriage. "Only two? Surely you'll stay a while?" he added anxiously.

"I only packed for a week's time—"

"A week? In only two cases? Mary, I knew you were a wonder, but now I know you are a saint."

Mrs. Pennett cleared her throat, and it was clear she thought an invitation into the house was appropriate. Godfrey raised suddenly sorrowful eyes to that impressive residence's facade, and sighed deeply. "Perhaps," he said with faint hope, "they would not notice if I slipped into your conveyance and we made straight-away back to London . . .?"

Mary's giggle and Mrs. Pennett's pursed lips put a period to that dream, so he took up Mary's hand and settled it on his arm. "Remember, later, that you asked for this," he warned, his expression more sadly resigned than even that of a basset hound.

As he led her up the steps she had a moment to take in his home. It was a beautiful, modern, white brick, three-story delight, set atop a slight rise. The grounds were not ancient, but it was clear that although many of the shrubberies were only ten or twenty years in place, a great deal of the aged trees had been retained, lending the property grace and charm. There was a duck pond to the left, shaded by lazy trees that stooped to drag their leaves across the water's surface. To the right, barely perceptible behind the house itself must surely be the stables, also in shining white brick. Columns of looming white graced the front of his home, and the large windows were accented by shutters painted in a soft gray shade, behind which she glimpsed pale blue silk curtains. "Godfrey," she breathed reverently. "It's beautiful."

"Yes," he said, his mouth quirking into an almost-smile. "And deceptively peaceful in its appearance."

As he pushed open one of the two large front doors, she was met at once by a loud hum of noise. She had only a moment to take in the large foyer, complete with black and white marble tiles on the floor and a spectacular crystal chandelier, before Godfrey had led her to a room at the diagonal from the entrance, from which emanated the hubbub.

They stood for a moment in the doorway, and Mary felt her eyes grow wide as she realized that there must be as many as twenty females within. They were dressed in varying shades and hues, looking for all the world like a human flower garden scattered over the rugs and settees within. Although the sound level was rather high, it only took Godfrey's gentle clearing of his throat to bring all eyes their way, and an immediate end to all speech.

"My family," he intoned rather formally, "I should like for you to meet my very dearest friend, Lady Mary Wagnall."

A chorus of 'how-do-you-dos' filled the room, followed by another echoing silence.

"And this is her companion, Mrs. Pennett," Godfrey said, stepping into the room with Mary at his side, enough to let Mrs. Pennett step forward and make her curtsy.

Another chorus of murmured greetings filled the room, but not one pair of eyes wandered from Godfrey, as they all sat and awaited further enlightenment.

"Mary," Godfrey said as he stepped further into the room, his hand over hers where it lay on his arm. Mrs. Pennett followed in their wake. He led them toward the eldest female in the room. "This is my mother, Lady Sarah Rothayne."

"My dear, how pleasant to meet you. Godfrey has told us of his new friend. We are so glad you could join us."

"I pray it is no bother—"

"Not at all. You can see for yourself we are quite used to company," Lady Rothayne said, indicating the crowded room with a movement of her hand. "We have a pair of rooms ready for you and for Mrs. Pennett."

"Thank you," Mary said. Mrs. Pennett, looking a trifle awed, made a second acknowledging curtsy.

"Now, if you would all be so good as to allow me to point," Godfrey said by way of apology for the crudity, and proceeded to do just that. "This lady here is Hortense. She is our eldest, and would not thank me for telling you how much so." He received a disdainful look down that lady's nose, upon which perched a set of spectacles, for his trouble. He proceeded, "In age order, then, there is Eugenia, Angela, Marian, Penelope, Sofie—that is short for Sophronia—Daphne, and the lovely lady in pink is my closest-in-age sibling, Georgette, the new mother. I, alas, am the younger brother of all eight of them." He paused to take a breath, then went on, "My nieces then. Hortenses's four: Ann, Margaret, Lorraine, and Elizabeth. Eugenia's three: Karen, Marcia, and Stephanie. Here we have Angela's two darlings: Katherine and Suzanne. Marian and Penelope each have the one daughter, respectively Alice and Rosina. Sofie is our newlywed, and has had the bad manners to have not yet seen to her 'duty' by way of producing any offspring for our already oversized family."

This comment caused that lady to fluster a little, but Godfrey, as usual, went blithely on. "And of course you see our newest, Jessica, there in her mother's arms. That, as your math will tell you, makes me the slave of twenty-one females."

"How do you do?" Mary said to the room at large, already quite lost as to who was who, except for

Sofie, who was the only other sibling to have the auburn-tinted hair. They were all handsome people, a revelation which made Mary feel just the tiniest bit plainer than usual.

"Are you two going to be married?" the eldest niece, Ann, asked abruptly.

"Good heavens, no!" Godfrey replied, aghast. "I tell you, Mary is my friend. I could not do *that* to a friend."

"Quite right," someone said.

"We despair of him, Mary," Sofie, the one with hair like Godfrey's, explained. "We wish for him to marry. It is his duty. He *is* the duke. But none of us is willing to sacrifice a friend to such a state of being, and equally none of us wishes to see someone for whom we do not care become the mistress of the house. It is a dilemma, I declare."

"And I, of course, do not care to marry at all, but they do not listen to me," Godfrey said in mock weariness, or at least Mary thought he was mocking.

"But you *must* marry someday," one cried.

"Of course he must," cried another of his sister's.

"He will. He just likes to tease us so."

"Well, I for one pity the girl."

"Yes, it would be a hard life having to make a go of it with one such as Godfrey."

"To say nothing of having to deal with all of you," he jumped in with a rather sour look about his mouth.

"Posh."

"How he does go on."

"Well!" Godfrey cried with that over-bright manner of one who wishes to make an escape. "I must see to getting Mary settled in her room. Good host duties, and all that! In fact, then I think I'll show her about the place. We'll see you all at suppertime." Abruptly he turned, his hand still tightly over Mary's, forcing her to throw her thanks over her shoulder as he marched her from the room.

He did not let her stop until they had flown up the wide sloping staircase. There on the landing he paused long enough to take a deep, relieved breath, and then turned to Mrs. Pennett, who followed in their tracks. "You will see that your mistress's bags are safely ensconced?" he asked pleasantly, though it was no less than a command.

Mrs. Pennett gave in gracefully, simply inclining her head before she slipped back down the stairs.

Smiling, Godfrey turned his attention to Mary to ask, "Are you ready to meet still more of my relatives?"

She nodded somewhat bemusedly, wondering if he meant a grandmother or great-aunt who was confined to her room. He led her down a long corridor filled with a variety of paintings and marble busts in small alcoves, past a number of doors, some open, some closed, and through the closed one at the end of the long corridor. "Gentlemen," Godfrey said by way of a greeting, as four men of differing ages turned toward him.

Mary's eyes flew to Godfrey's face. "You did not quite write me all the truth, Godfrey. How silly of me not to figure it out for myself!" she cried, for of course these must be his sister's husbands. Although it was true he was surrounded by females, here then were also some males with whom he could take refuge.

"Would you have come if you'd known I had *some* relief?" he said quietly near her ear.

The eldest of the four, his hair streaked with gray at the temples and in his beard, stepped forward as he transferred a brandy glass from his right hand to the other. "So this must be Mary," he said in a soft, well-modulated voice.

"She is. Gentlemen, may I make known to you my very good friend, Lady Mary Wagnall. Mary, this is Sir Edmund Billings, Hortense's fellow."

"How do you do?" Edmund asked politely, gently taking the gloved hand she offered him.

The other three gents stepped forward as she gave her polite answer, each offering their hand in turn to hers as Godfrey introduced them. "This scalawag is Lord Timothy Gateway, shackled to Angela, and this is Mr. Aaron Seffixhenny, the new bridegroom among us. That makes him Sofie's lucky fellow. And here is little Jessica's papa, Lord Kevin Withal."

"Congratulations are in order, my lord," Mary said in his direction as she made a curtsy to them all.

"Thank you, Lady Wagnall. I must say, we were not surprised the babe was yet another female to come among us."

"We Rothaynes are stubborn, even in the matter of procreation," Godfrey quipped.

Edmund lifted his eyebrows, followed by a glance toward Mary at the scandalous comment. When she did not blush, nor in any wise seem discomfited, he chose to do nothing himself, not even bothering to frown upon Godfrey. That fellow had boasted 'his Mary' was a most unusual female, and already Edmund had a sense of what he meant, for this was no brazen tart, but a refined lady, and yet there she was, already engaged in speech with his two other brothers-in-law, no sign of awkwardness about her. Good. One did grow so weary of giggling misses straight from the schoolroom who could not put two coherent words together in a sentence. And one grew equally weary of the parade belowstairs, for *those* ladies had no problem putting any number of words together, not even allowing one a pause in which to respond. A little bit of unfamilial gentility was quite the respite.

Edmund moved to Godfrey's side, close enough to say in a low voice, "I must say, I think I shall like this Mary of yours, even though we have but met."

"And I will tell you that what you have met is what she is, sir, a paragon."

"A virtuous one?" Edmund asked.

Godfrey turned to throw him a dark look, but then he saw at once that Edmund had not meant to be unkind; he was merely prying. That kind of behavior was surely reprehensible, but one grew used to its like here. Godfrey put on a pained face, sighed heavily, and replied, "I fear so."

Edmund smiled mildly, and made no attempt to hide the fact that this conversation would be related to his wife, as he commented, "I do not know if Hortense will be happy to know that or not."

"She will say she is, as only vows before a preacher would satisfy that one, but inside she will be regretting that Lady Mary does not have that avenue by which to ensnare me. A marriage by compromise is still a marriage. That would be Hortense's thought."

"Why don't you settle down, old chap? It's not so bad."

"Yes, why don't you?" Mary asked as she approached them, the three other husbands in her wake, their conversation having come to an end, so that now all eyes were fixed upon Godfrey.

"It is impolite to eavesdrop," Godfrey responded lightly.

"It is impolite to talk quietly while in a group," Mary countered. "Or in your case, not so quietly."

He allowed his eyes to fall meaningfully toward the floor, and in the silence that filled the room they all clearly heard the babble from belowstairs. "It is," he said, his tone having grown weighty, "my sincere belief that I should beget nothing but more females. Acres and acres of females. You must all see, then, why I forebear."

It was Mary who began to laugh first, but she was quickly joined by all the rest, even Godfrey.

They poured her a glass of ratafia, settled her in a chair, queried her as to her journey, and proceeded on to telling tales of the horrors of living or visiting among the "Rothayne Bevy".

"Harry, Stephen, and Eric—they're the clever ones. They all found excuses not to come. And of course, there's Humphrey, who's away at sea more times than not," Lord Timothy explained about the other missing brothers-in-law.

"Sofie said she wouldn't come without me, the roads being unsafe with brigands and all," Aaron put in, looking glum.

"But escape *is* possible. We ride a bit, don't we, fellows?" Godfrey said. At their nods he went on, "Every morning at eight. Would you care to join us, Mary?"

"Oh yes, I should like that!" she cried, her face shining under all the attention that was being lavished on her, and at their eager looks of invitation.

"Then let's away to the stable, to find you the proper nag," Edmund said, setting down his snifter.

A movement at the door halted them in their steps, for it was Lady Rothayne who stood there. "Godfrey," she said with faint disapproval, "I thought you were seeing Lady Wagnall to her room, and yet I am told this has not occurred."

Godfrey threw a regretful look about the room, gave Mary a half-shrug, and declared, "We were going there just now, Mama."

"Via the stables?" she asked politely but with a touch of iron in her tone.

" 'Twould be a curious path, now, wouldn't it?" Godfrey said smoothly, turning to offer Mary his arm.

She stepped next to him, slipping her hand onto his arm.

"Lead the way," she said up at him.

As they followed his mother down the long corridor, he said *sotto voce,* "Don't let them monopolize you! Save me some time! Say you will, I beg of you."

"It's why I came, Godfrey," she assured him, unable to suppress the soft smile that came to play around her lips. It was a great, good feeling to be wanted.

When he left her at the door of her room, wherein she was accompanied by his mother, she could not help but notice how cool the room seemed. It was not that it was one iota cooler than the corridor, she knew with a sigh, it was that Godfrey was gone from her side. *Oh, I must be careful here,* she thought to herself. *He is the beautiful window, but not the life-giving sun,* she reminded herself.

"My dear, is the room not satisfactory?" Lady Rothayne asked, interrupting her thoughts.

Mary turned to face the silver-haired lady, a little flustered at being caught ruminating. "Oh, my, yes. I mean, no, it is a lovely room. I was merely wool-gathering. The length of the trip, I guess," she made hasty excuses.

"I know quite well how wearying travel can be, but fortunately dinner is to be served soon. That is always fortifying, I find, after travel. Although, I could have a tray sent up, if you feel the need for something now . . .?"

"No, thank you. You are most kind," Mary said, moving toward the large bed where her two cases lay, already emptied into the drawers of the dresser near the bed and the wardrobe, evidence that Mrs. Pennett had preceded her here. "I think I'll just rest until the supper hour is announced."

"That will be at six, my dear. We dine early in the

country," Lady Rothayne said, moving toward the door.

Mary lay down upon the bed, intending only to test its comfort level, but soon her mind was wandering, and not long after that she had in truth fallen asleep.

Chapter Eight

She awoke when a weight settled on the end of the bed. Blinking her eyes, she shifted up onto her elbows, trying to focus through the dim light at the invader. In a moment she saw that it was not a servant that had roused her, but Godfrey.

"The chambermaid said you were sleeping," he said quietly, a smile dancing in his light blue eyes.

"Oh, Godfrey, never say you let her know you were coming in my room!" she said, wanting to smile back at that perfect mouth even while consternation stirred in her voice.

"Of course I did. I may not come home often, but I have come often enough that the servants are used to my ways. But, look, dearest, I left the door open, so you are safe in person as well as in reputation. You do *want* to be safe, don't you? I *could* close the door, if—?"

"Godfrey," she cried, exasperated, swinging her legs over the side of the bed, even as she smiled a little.

"Come, you are only two minutes away from making the dinner hour late," he said, offering her his hand.

She stepped around the hand, moving to her mirror. "Oh no! Look at me! I have red creases on my face, my dress is wrinkled, my hair is a shambles—"

"Hush, darling. No one will care."

She looked at him in the mirror then, and he saw clearly what she was thinking: "Of course they will not care for I am not a beauty. Why do I need to worry about my appearance?" Angrily he gave a quick shake of his head, denying the statement in her eyes. It filled his chest with a sudden and peculiar burning sensation to see that knowing look in her eyes, that bald statement, for he had seen it before, and to see it as truth again in her eyes brought him a sudden and undeniable anger. Why had she been made to feel inferior? What comments had family or 'friends' sent her way to make her think she was less than fine—what some would call handsome—if not truly pretty? But perhaps that was part of what had first spoken to him at their meeting, this vulnerability of hers, so like unto his own. "I'll help you," he said, his deep voice so low as to almost go unheard.

He reached for the back of her dress and began undoing buttons.

"Godfrey, no!"

"Hush, it's only buttons. Quickly now, before the chambermaid returns."

His warning worked, for with a quick, worried glance at the open door, she stood still and let his nimble fingers finish their work. "Now, change quickly, and I'll do up the new buttons for you." He moved to the door, and closed it behind himself.

In the corridor, he allowed one hand to shape into a fist, and a fierce scowl crossed his features for a moment before he was able to smother the anger that flared within. It was just that she had startled him, for he was only used to play and lightness in their acquaintance. Of course, she was as human as he, and it was not to be wondered at that she had received her share of unkindnesses. It was, alas, the way of the world, as he had learned himself not so very many years ago. And he, unlike many, had at least this cursedly handsome face to hide behind, he told himself, though a tiny voice also whispered that same face had in fact been the foundation from which had sprung his own woes.

Inside the room, she slid out of the dress even as she moved toward the wardrobe. None of the dresses she had brought had, of course, yet been pressed back into a premium condition, but the light blue sarcenet was not too wrinkled, so she took that one down quickly. She was dressed in it in a moment, and she struggled for a vigorous five minutes more, trying to do most of the buttons herself, but finally she had to move to the door and whisper, "Godfrey?"

He came back in at once, almost striking her with the door in his haste. "Mama will be sending someone for you any minute," he warned even as he put his hands on her shoulders and turned her around, his fingers going at once to the buttons left unfastened. He was swiftly done, his hands shifting up to her hair to begin pulling pins. "Now, as to your hair, can you do it yourself?"

She nodded, making his fingers dance accidentally across the back of her head, tingling her scalp so that she shivered. "It won't be grand, but I can get it up in a tidy knot," she said in a voice that was not quite steady.

"Looser than a knot, love, please. That chestnut color must be softly set to be of advantage."

She nodded again, to cover the fact that she shivered yet again, and he slipped from the room. She snatched up her brush, which she applied with hurried vigor to her hair, and it was not until she was fastening a tidy if inexpert chignon that she realized her fingers were trembling.

When she cracked open the door to her bedroom, she gave a little sigh of relief, for Godfrey was not there. His absence gave her that much longer to compose herself. It was, she told herself, only natural that she should be flustered at the kind of personal attentions he had given her. She should have insisted that he ring for the chambermaid, that the girl could serve her well enough. Why hadn't she done that? Yes, it would have taken longer and made her especially late, but that was the way of things. Oh, he had overridden her, as usual! It was his way. Yes, it was his way, she told herself as she clenched her hands into her skirts, trying to steady them there.

Her color was a little high when she joined the others in the dining room, lending her a certain dramatic presence, if only she had known it.

The decorous way she moved, the way her head was held high, they were all the marks of a true lady, Edmund thought to himself, underscoring yet again his decision to like this female.

Timothy had no thought as to why he was pleased to be seated on Lady Wagnall's right, but he was, and Aaron was quick to get a lively conversation started with the lady concerning the use of tigers versus ostlers.

After a few moments of quiet, refined conversation, the veneer of polite society fell away, and the usual hubbub resumed. The two eldest nieces, Ann and Karen, sixteen and fifteen years of age respectively, had been invited to the table. They looked charming in their white, ruffled dresses, pleased to find they were not to be counted among all the remaining cousins who were confined to the nursery to partake of their suppers there. That meant there were fifteen people seated at table, with Georgette not attending as she was still taking her meals in her room following the birth.

"Vulgar lot, aren't they?" Godfrey said loudly toward Mary, who was five chairs away from where he sat at the head of the long mahogany table.

"Homey, I should say," Mary responded with a warm smile for everyone's benefit.

"You are too kind," Godfrey said with emphasis. No one bothered to be the slightest bit quieter, though it was clear they listened with relish to whatever conversation they could when they themselves were not speaking. "I swear I shall never be seen in public with the lot of them."

Mary, quite unused to a meal being such an unstructured occasion, began to giggle, having to hide the act behind her napkin, but no one took her shaking shoulders amiss, so finally she was able to recover her poise, although a grin lingered on her lips.

"Lady Wagnall!" Aaron shouted at her. "Just wanted you to know it's not this way at our home," he cried, pointing from himself to his wife, Sofie. "Just seems to happen here. No one tries to fight against it. Lost cause, and all that!"

"I see!" she shouted back.

Just then Godfrey raised a silver fork and rapped his water goblet with ringing effect. The table fell silent as all eyes turned his way. He looked down both lengths of the table, and toward his mother at the far end, and said with a look of satisfaction, "Just wanted to see if it still worked."

"Oh, Godfrey!" his mother scolded mildly, and then the din rose swiftly again to its previous level.

Mary found herself partaking of the most hilarious meal she had ever had. The food itself was delicious, the conversation fascinating, and the experience of dining *ala Rothayne* (as Godfrey put it) uniquely charming. There was no pretense, and the laughter was genuine, not polite. It was deemed appropriate to tease lightly, including even, quite apparently, guests. After several shocked blushes, Mary found herself giving as good as she got. At one point all the gentlemen engaged in a lengthy discourse on how inappropriate the name 'Mary'—which means 'bitterness'—was for their guest. This led to a spirited discussion of which of the local bitters was to be preferred, and hence to Aaron's tale of a misspent night in a pub, cleverly told by that fine fellow until Godfrey was shaking so hard with laughter that he actually laid his head on his arm on the table, thumping the surface with his other hand in time to his gales of laughter. Mary laughed with him, and the whole table, until she had to hold her side and her mouth actually hurt from being so long upturned. Oh, it was so vulgar, so unrefined, this raucous gathering, and she adored every minute of it. She did not want to leave the table, even after the last possible crumb of marzipan had been tucked within the last viable pair of lips, even after the last sip of wine had been drained from the last cup. She could have sat there the whole night through, soaking up the goodwill and companionship that these people so freely offered her, an outsider. It was enough for them that Godfrey had named her 'friend.' It was enough for her that they found her worthy of the title.

Finally, though, as is the way of the world, the gaiety fell away, replaced by the more normal conversational bits about who needed to go where the next day, and who was to make their departures soon, did the grey mare need to be shoed again, how was that new footman working out, and the like. The hubbub died down to a moderate level, and people began to trade chairs, so that the women gravitated down to one end of the table, and the men to the other. Mary lifted a quiet eyebrow at this, accustomed as she was to the removal of the gents to their port, usually in a room far removed from their womenfolk. She herself made no move, but she turned in the direction of the men, trying to catch snatches of their conversation without looking too forward, while at the same time having one ear pointed toward the sometimes intriguing comments of the women.

She heard tell of a rodent problem at the mill that had increased with the floodings, and she heard Lady Rothayne discussing when Georgette might again attend church services. She heard that the war department was rebuilding their ranks, and she learned that Eugenia had detested the daughter of the near neighbors ever since her fifth birthday party. When Godfrey spoke of revisiting the vicar to see how the poorer lot were getting on and what might be done for them, she nodded approvingly to herself, and when she heard Lady Rothayne say the same thing, she ventured to speak up and point out that plans were being laid at both ends of the table in that quarter.

"Would you, Godfrey? I daresay that the vicar appreciates your concern," Lady Rothayne also nodded approvingly.

"We must do something for those families, for there will be no harvesting this fall, no jobs for them," he responded soberly.

Mary gazed upon her friend, unused to seeing him in the role of landowner, and therefore without the light of amusement dancing in his eyes. The somber expression on his face took not one whit away from his beauty, and in fact only served to point up his similarity to the carved angels that one admired so on the cathedrals, their faces beautiful with the gravity of their love for God, and what could only be their disappointment with erring man. She gathered her hands together in her lap, for of a sudden she wished nothing so much as to cross to his side and soothe the solemnity from his brow with her hands. She wished to whisper something in his ear to make him smile, to somehow, even for the space of a few minutes, spare him the worries of the world, this world, his home and income, his people and his family.

But then that impulse faded, gone as swiftly as it had been born, and she wanted nothing so much as to weep, for she found her heart was swelling with joy, the joy of finding something of precious value in a deep, dark well. It was not that it was unexpected, not at all, for she had liked him from the moment they had met, and she knew she could never like a total scoundrel. No, it was not unexpected, but still it took her breath away, and filled her with pride, to see so clearly written upon his extraordinary face that he cared. He cared for these women — even if they nearly drove him mad — and he cared for the people that relied on him for their income, even for the roofs over their heads. He cared that people

104

might go hungry. He cared that he had yet another niece to claim as family. He cared that the soil held under his titled name must be worked properly and made productive. The *ennui,* the blatant disregard of societal rules, the ways and means of the town man were not the sum total of the whole man. He had more than one side to him, and as amusing as the town man was, it was this farm fellow that would stand steady when the need arose. Yes, he was still the sleek, pleasure-seeking cat, but like the cat he would defend what was his, would prowl his territory relentlessly, staving off whatever dangers might stalk him and his.

Mary was so moved by the not-quite-unexpected discovery of her friend's depth that she could not raise her eyes, staring down at her empty plate and blinking furiously, willing away the tears that she could never explain were they to fall. Gradually she became aware of the dialogue going back and forth around her, and forced her ears to listen, to concentrate on something other than the large lump in her throat.

"Mama, I don't believe this is quite the thing to discuss at the table," she heard Godfrey say. Although he still had the sober look about him, there was a pinched look about him now too, perhaps a sign of embarrassment or annoyance.

"Godfrey, she is the prettiest thing. She is educated, clever, well thought of in these parts. No one can fault her in the slightest. I have seen for myself that you were not indifferent to the girl. I have tried to fathom, very indirectly of course, whether or not the girl and her family are receptive, and I believe I can truly say that not only are they receptive, but possibly even eager," Lady Rothayne said.

Eugenia nodded sagely, adding, "Although she has not had to run a household herself yet, I am sure her mother is the kind to train her daughters—"

"And have you seen her embroidery work? She sews like a dream!" Hortense interrupted, her sisters nodding around her.

Mary glanced at Godfrey's face, which seemed to be composed, but she saw the blue lightning in his eyes, and wondered that the others did not. Perhaps they chose to ignore it.

"And she can paint. Have you seen the large canvas in their front hall? *She* painted that! Oh, I'll grant it's not a Rembrandt, but one has to admit that it's rather finely done," Penelope called across the table.

Angela threw in, "And she plays the pianoforte quite charmingly. Do you recall that musicale evening, oh, about two months ago? I thought to myself, well, goodness, the girl has some little talent—"

"That's quite enough!" Godfrey growled loudly, suddenly pushing back his chair. His face was finally touched with two dull spots of red as he tugged down his waistcoat in a gesture of finality. "Gentlemen," he said to the room, but he did not wait for any response from them as he strode purposefully from the room, apparently in search of an after-dinner drink.

The ladies fell to exchanging comments, except for Hortense, who caught Mary's eye over the table. She rose smoothly and came to Mary's side. "Have you a shawl?" she asked.

Mary nodded.

"Then let us fetch it, and go for a walk in the gardens, shall we?" Hortense said calmly, politely, but there was that in her attitude which suggested a wish to talk.

"Of course," Mary agreed, intrigued.

They went to her room, found a shawl, got one for Hortense, and proceeded out the library doors into the garden.

"It is more chill than I had thought," Hortense said, frowning up at the dark clouds over their heads.

"At least it is not raining."

"It shall be doing so again, soon," Hortense sighed.

"That is old news indeed."

"I'm sorry about the way we are," the older woman said suddenly.

Mary shook her head, even as she asked, "You mean the enthusiasm at table? In truth, I cannot fault it. Who is there to offend? Personally I abhor stuffy dinners."

"Mary, it is quite evident to all of us why Godfrey has taken you to his heart: you are a truly good person. There are not many who would gloss over our very countrified ways, and instead turn them into some kind of virtue," Hortense said with sincere gravity, though one corner of her mouth quirked upward.

"Perhaps I am not so much kind as uncouth," Mary grinned.

"Touché!" Hortense laughed. But it was not for amusing banter that she had brought them to the gardens. She added without preamble, "You sensed that I wanted to talk to you?"

Mary nodded.

"About Godfrey, of course. About that little scene at table." She paused, glancing again at the clouds over their heads. "I'll speak simply, as I expect the rain to start again any moment."

"Please do."

"Mama was speaking of a young lady—Miss Yardley, by name—whom we have decided is the perfect wife for Godfrey."

Mary's heart suddenly contracted painfully. She had never thought about Godfrey marrying—which, of course, he must—as he had been so vehemently opposed to the idea. It was impossible to imagine his will being overridden by anyone else's, but it was with sharpened ears that she listened to the rest of Hortense's statements.

"You must understand something of our family to understand why it is that Godfrey has not already settled down. You see, our father, as fortune would have it, was the sort of man who truly enjoyed the company of women. He was, therefore, the happiest of men to be surrounded by what he affectionately termed his 'harem'. Godfrey decries the fact that he was an only son, but I, for one, am glad there were no others. I believe it was only Godfrey's singularity that made him stand out to our father at all, besides the simple fact that a man must declare an heir, and that it is preferred that such an heir be one of his own making. Father would, I believe, have let any number of sons go willy-nilly, preferring the company of his daughters. And what kind of life would that have been? No, Godfrey was very fortunate to be born the last and only male.

"It is not surprising, therefore, that Godfrey grew up in his father's shadow, learning to enjoy, admire, cherish, and seek our company by virtue of it being his only choice, and his only example. I feel safe in saying that to him we were all just a little shy of goddesses, for we were older, we were overbearing, and we were catered to in all our whims by Mother and Father both. How else could the lad think?

"And all would have been well, except, of course, that he must go out into the real world. Out there, as you may imagine, he met females who loved his beauty, but not his soul. If but one had wounded him, he should have rallied and been satisfied to keep the majority of womankind on the pedestals Father had so effectively erected for us, but there were a series of cruelties and broken promises, if not broken hearts, and I am afraid that the goddesses were proved to have feet of clay."

"It is hard to imagine Godfrey with a broken heart," Mary said uncertainly, her own beginning to ache painfully in sympathy.

"Oh, he is recovered, in most respects. At least well enough that we think the time has come. We think that because he is who he is, and because he is not exactly a lad of tender years anymore, it is time a woman who would satisfy us all be found. A tall order, indeed, I may assure you!

"As you must know, our Godfrey is a clever fellow. At first, when the pain of knowledge was new, his tongue was sharp to keep people away, to not let them see his vulnerability. It earned him that atrocious nickname, 'The Blade', although even I must admit that at the time it was not unwarranted, for he could cut you easily with that quick wit of his. But, like most of us, what had once been needed, is now perhaps ready to be discarded. We think, finally, that the opportunity and the time are right. The bitterness has softened, the acid tongue now comes to the fore only to take on an oaf, or any of the low-minded kinds whom he has never suffered gladly."

"That is true enough."

"Then you also know that he is not cruel or un-kind. He may show up unannounced at a party, but he would never snub the daughter of the house, no matter how unattractive or stupid she may be. He would not think to tease or jest about another's in-firmity or physical being. Why, I have a friend who has two different colored eyes, and he never—in the twenty years she has been my friend—has ever men-tioned the fact. Godfrey may not have many virtues, but forbearance and tact are his. He may drink until he cannot walk, but he would never encourage a raw lad to do the same. He himself would remain sober, if only to see that the fellow made it home safely, and with his purse still in his pocket and his life not threatened by his own inability to guide a horse."

"Yes, it's true," Mary said.

Hortense did not miss the glitter in the younger woman's eyes, and for a moment fell silent.

"Go on," Mary encouraged her, for now she had to hear it all. She was learning so much about the man, and there was nothing she did not want to know. Godfrey had ever been a sullied angel; the knowledge of his trials would only bind her affection the more to him.

"Yes, well. So you see, Godfrey has decided, al-though he would deny it entirely, that only a certain manner of female will do to be his wife. Oh, she need not be rich, nor especially pretty, but there are many other things she *must* be."

"Yes?" Mary said in a soft, almost whispered voice, a picture forming in her mind of this proposed candidate, this Miss Yardley.

"She must be a 'good woman', well respected by her community. She must carry no taint of scandal about her. And yet—and this is the dilemma—she must have her feet firmly planted on the soil. No churchwoman for Godfrey. A good woman, but not a saint. She must be capable of not only tolerating but appreciating his faults, of refraining from lectures, of . . ." she gave a discreet little cough, but went on despite the discomfort that had crept into her voice, ". . . she must be able to be just a little bit 'wayward', if you take my meaning."

"Wayward?" Mary echoed, though she understood well enough. One did not arrive at the age of 28 without understanding something of the world.

"He could never have a wife who . . . who was . . . well, *cool* toward him. You see, he is, despite it all, a romantic. He wishes to be loved . . . and desired. It is, after all, what he was raised to expect from our kind, and roots will call us back, as they say." She cleared her throat again daintily, hastily going on, "Of course, he would deny it all. He would laugh at me for saying such things aloud, but I believe them the truth." She smiled a little around the eyes, and poked a little gentle fun at herself, "I do have the advantage of a few more years experience than he."

Mary's feet slowed to a stop. "This Miss Yardley . . . you believe she is all those things? You—who have tried for years—believe that now you have found the one who Godfrey will accept?"

"Yes, I do," Hortense said, slipping an arm through Mary's to turn her back toward the house. A single drop of rain had hit upon her glasses, Mary could see as they turned. She stared at it for a moment, for it seemed such a perfect reflection of an inexplicable heaviness in her chest, flowing downward, and making her limbs feel weak and weary.

"Miss Yardley is quite right for the position. None of us dislikes her, and then again none of us is particularly friendly with her. You see, Godfrey has refused the company of several candidates before this day, I can tell you, and since they were our friends, it was not always a comfortable thing, these rejections of his. But Miss Yardley is not the friend of anyone in the household, though she is an inoffensive creature entirely. She is very pretty, yet living in the shadow of her father's brother's piety, she has garnered no reputation for impiety herself. She gives every sign of understanding the duties a wife performs for a household. She has the added advantage of being rather young, so although she has been properly raised, she is still, well 'impressionable', shall we say? She is at exactly the perfect moment in her life where she has yet to choose which manner will be her own. She could be influenced easily, and how better to be influenced than by a man who only wants to make an honest and loving bargain with her?

"Furthermore, she would be living here, most of the year, in the very community that knows her. She would surely acquire the kind of town polish that Godfrey would care for, and yet, too, she would be primarily amongst the very people who could see to it that she was not corrupted entirely," Hortense finished with a satisfied nod of her head.

Mary stared at the older woman. She knew the woman did not mean to sound so calculating, and she also knew that it was perfectly normal for families to involve themselves in the making of such marriages. It was in fact more times than not how it was done. If anything, Hortense and her sisters and mother were being considerate, allowing that God-

MORE PASSION AND ADVENTURE AWAIT... YOUR TRIP TO A BIG ADVENTUROUS WORLD BEGINS WHEN YOU ACCEPT YOUR FIRST 4 NOVELS ABSOLUTELY *FREE*
(AN $18.00 VALUE)

Accept your Free gift and start to experience more of the passion and adventure you like in a historical romance novel. Each Zebra novel is filled with proud men, spirited women and tempestuous love that you'll remember long after you turn the last page.

Zebra Historical Romances are the finest novels of their kind. They are written by authors who really know how to weave tales of romance and adventure in the historical settings you love. You'll feel like you've actually gone back in time with the thrilling stories that each Zebra novel offers.

GET YOUR FREE GIFT WITH THE START OF YOUR HOME SUBSCRIPTION

Our readers tell us that these books sell out very fast in book stores and often they miss the newest titles. So Zebra has made arrangements for you to receive the four newest novels published each month.

You'll be guaranteed that you'll never miss a title, and home delivery is so convenient. And to show you just how easy it is to get Zebra Historical Romances, we'll send you your first 4 books absolutely FREE! Our gift to you just for trying our home subscription service.

BIG SAVINGS AND FREE HOME DELIVERY

Each month, you'll receive the four newest titles as soon as they are published. You'll probably receive them even before the bookstores do. What's more, you may preview these exciting novels free for 10 days. If you like them as much as we think you will, just pay the low preferred subscriber's price of just $3.75 each. *You'll save $3.00 each month off the publisher's price.* AND, your savings are even greater because there are never any shipping, handling or other hidden charges—FREE Home Delivery. Of course you can return any shipment within 10 days for full credit, no questions asked. There is no minimum number of books you must buy.

4 FREE BOOKS

TO GET YOUR 4 FREE BOOKS WORTH $18.00 — MAIL IN THE FREE BOOK CERTIFICATE T O D A Y

Fill in the Free Book Certificate below, and we'll send your FREE BOOKS to you as soon as we receive it.

If the certificate is missing below, write to: Zebra Home Subscription Service, Inc., P.O. Box 5214, 120 Brighton Road, Clifton, New Jersey 07015-5214.

FREE BOOK CERTIFICATE

4 FREE BOOKS

ZEBRA HOME SUBSCRIPTION SERVICE, INC.

YES! Please start my subscription to Zebra Historical Romances and send me my first 4 books absolutely FREE. I understand that each month I may preview four new Zebra Historical Romances free for 10 days. If I'm not satisfied with them, I may return the four books within 10 days and owe nothing. Otherwise, I will pay the low preferred subscriber's price of just $3.75 each; a total of $15.00, *a savings off the publisher's price of $3.00.* I may return any shipment and I may cancel this subscription at any time. There is no obligation to buy any shipment and there are no shipping, handling or other hidden charges. Regardless of what I decide, the four free books are mine to keep.

NAME _____

ADDRESS _____ APT _____

CITY _____ STATE _____ ZIP _____

TELEPHONE ( ) _____

SIGNATURE _____ (if under 18, parent or guardian must sign)

GET
FOUR
FREE
BOOKS

(AN $18.00 VALUE)

frey must have a marriage of which he approved if that is what he desired. "Why tell *me* all these things?" she asked, hearing the heaviness in her own voice.

"For the simple reason that I wish to enlist your assistance," Hortense said. Her arm pulled gently at Mary's, hurrying her toward the house as more drops began to patter around them.

"My assistance?" Would she ever stop sounding so simple, repeating everything Hortense said? What was wrong with her? Had she taken a chill? She tried to shake off the lethargy that filled her, aware that not even her quick steps had served to clear her slow mind.

"You are the closest to Godfrey. He listens to you as he listens to no other female these days. You must be the one to persuade him of Miss Yardley's virtues. You must be the one that edges him into that lady's company. I know you love him even as we all do, and I know that you would wish him happily settled."

"Of course, but . . . I don't know . . ." she faltered. "Godfrey and I are never serious for a moment. I do not think he would care to have me dictating to him—"

"You underestimate yourself, but perhaps that is because you have not known Godfrey all that long. I tell you, you have the fellow's ear. You have but to whisper, subtly, in that ear and he will be as complaisant as a lamb, I vow it," Hortense said, a satisfied light coming into her eyes.

"But he might begin to dislike me if he ever suspected!" Mary wailed, appalled at the very thought.

"It is a risk, but only if you are less clever than I think you are."

"I could not bear it — !"

Hortense heard the dread in the other woman's voice, so she pressed her point. "And do you care to see Godfrey grow old, an aged bachelor with no family, no heir, no affections to warm his long winter evenings?"

"He would have all of you," Mary argued feebly, her resistance already crumbling at the thought of Godfrey never having that which all men must surely, if secretly, aspire to. Of course he must have a spouse, and children. He must have them to bring him happiness . . . even as she must.

"Posh!" Hortense said dismissively. "We give him fits. No, it's a family of his own that will make him happy."

And Mary knew it was true, for hadn't she been chasing that same dream herself for some time now, to find a family of her own? And what were those moments when he looked away from her, when his mouth tightened and he would not meet her eye? What had caused him to dread the very thing that Hortense assured her he longed for?

"You are right," she said, casting off her indecisive manner with an effort. "I would meet this Miss Yardley, and if she is half so suitable as you imply, then of course I will use what little influence I have with Godfrey in that regard."

"Good girl!" Hortense crowed just as they stepped onto the paving stones of the veranda that led into the house.

It had been raining for so long now that no one bothered to ask the ladies why they had chosen to walk in inclement weather. The men had not returned from their port, and in a short while Mary pleaded sleepiness. She retired to her room to lie on

114

her bed until Mrs. Pennett tapped at her door and entered.

"You're abed early," that lady said.

"I don't feel very well," Mary half-lied.

"Well, it's this country air, no doubt," Mrs. Pennett said with a sniff that showed she was being sarcastic. "It's a good thing we're bound back for London in just a matter of days."

Mary heard the warning tones, and winced to think that Mrs. Pennett might be guessing at the internal turmoil that even Mary did not want to think about too clearly. "Six days," she replied, and it was a kind of agreement with the companion.

Mrs. Pennett clucked around her charge, saw her tucked into bed, and left her to stare listlessly at the ceiling for a goodly portion of the night.

Chapter Nine

It came as no surprise to Mary when she learned the next day that an evening of card playing was being arranged, and that Miss Yardley was to be invited. Lady Rothayne wanted it to be held in one week, but Hortense — with a quick glance at Mary, who was to stay only five more days — talked her mother into holding it only two days hence.

"Two days! Impossible, not to mention rude!" her mother had cried, but Hortense had persuaded her that the invited guests would leap at any opportunity to be out and about, due to the incessant rain and the otherwise complete lack of activity.

Which, in fact, proved to be the case. By that same afternoon, all the invitations had been answered, with only the vicar declining, as he had a clerical assembly to attend outside of the village that night.

Mary sat with Hortense, marveling over the rapid success of the endeavor, when suddenly Godfrey put his head in at the door. She had not seen him since he had stomped from the table, and once again, as always, his handsome features made her pause in both deed and thought.

"Mary, come, please. We have something to discuss," he said, completely ignoring his sister.

She rose at once, and only later realized she had not offered any kind of parting to Hortense.

Once in the hall, he took her hand and placed it on his arm, and said in a low voice, "You did not ride with us this morning."

She lowered her head, and mumbled, "I wasn't sure—"

"That is Mama's fault, for interrupting us that first day. But you should have known I went ahead and picked a lovely little mare for you." His tone was faintly scolding.

"Yes, I should have known that."

"But now I have stolen you away from my greedy sisters, and I mean to keep you with me the better part of the day. What do you say to an afternoon ride then?"

It was raining, not too heavily, but not lightly either. The wind was up, and the clouds were heavy, promising no reprise. "I should like that very much!" she said, for what was weather when she was beside her 'beautiful window'?

He placed his hand over hers and squeezed lightly. "Good! We must go out, for there is no place where one is not disturbed in this household. Do you need to change?"

"I'll only be a moment," she assured him.

"Let me go up with you and guard your door, elsewise I know someone will steal you away yet again. And if I catch sight of your companion, I mean to steer your precious Mrs. Pennett away. She is not to come with us."

Since Mrs. Pennett was nothing less than an atrocious horsewoman, Mary acquiesced at once, or at least that is why she told herself she would not argue the point. "Yes," she said, and shivered, and vowed he would not undo her buttons yet again.

He escorted her to her room, where they found one of the maids straightening up. Mary at once solicited the girl's assistance, and with her help she was dressed in a trice, even to a sweet little riding bonnet tied cheerily under her chin, its maroon velvet ribbon matching her habit.

As soon as she opened her door, Godfrey's hand sprang forward, catching up her own. "There are dragons afoot!" he declared. His long legs strode purposefully toward the rear of the house, down a flight of stairs, and out the back entrance. Mary had to all but run to keep up with him. As they crossed the lawn to the stables, he flung a triumphant look back over his shoulder at her. "We are almost escaped! But trust me, continued haste is our only friend."

Inside the stable he instructed the groom to ready a horse for him, and he set about saddling the proposed mare for Mary. "Her name is Dumpling, which suits her personality as well as her girth," he told her. "She is Daphne's favorite, and Daphne is the most timid horsewoman among us, so I suspect Dumpling will give you no trouble."

"Oh, I am not afraid of horses. I rather like a spirited mount, at least in the country where they may run a bit."

"I ought to have known," he said as he pushed hard against the mare's side. When the creature exhaled noisily, he quickly cinched the girth strap tight. "A mere horse could not frighten my Mary, not when she is not frightened of me."

"I never was," she said, smiling. "I suppose it is because you have never played The Blade with me."

He moved to where he could offer her a hand up. She stepped forward and placed her booted foot in his cupped hands, and he threw her easily up into the sidesaddle. He patted the horse's neck, and said musingly, "So I haven't. Be glad, for that means you are neither a fool nor an idiot. I should have let you know if you were."

"But what will become of our friendship when I *do* do something foolish or idiotic?" she asked, looking down at him, half-afraid he meant what he said.

"Nothing, of course. For if I cut you up, why, you shall simply remember your stay here amongst my kin, and you will laugh heartily and know who the real fool is." He grinned up at her, instantly erasing the worried furrow that had crossed her brow.

"Coddled perhaps, but never a fool. A man cannot help the relations he must claim."

"I suppose I must claim them. I have been thinking of some way around the matter, but I confess I have not found it." The groom led the Duke's horse forward, holding the head while Godfrey mounted. Just then another groom came hastily around the corner and through the stable door. "M'lord," he cried, "I'se to fetch ye ta m'lady."

Godfrey's eyes widened in feigned horror, and he cried to Mary, "Away, I say! Let us flee! I never heard the summons, did you?"

"What summons?" she laughed as they put their heels to their mounts and sprang out through the stable doors.

They let the horses have their heads for a few minutes, both to put some distance behind them, and as a kind of payment for the startle they had given the poor beasts. The rain slashed into Mary's face and tore at her pelisse, and the wind pushed her hat from off her head so that it hung from her neck by its ribbons, but it never entered her head to complain or insist that they turn back. It felt good to be outside and (in truth!) away from all the people who inhabited Rothayne Manor. She began to realize that Godfrey's letters had not all been farce, but — given his role in this large family — based to a certain degree on truth. She could only be glad she had come, if only to allow him the excuses to find a little time for himself.

After a while he pulled back on the reins, and she followed suit. He edged his animal closer to hers, that he might not have to shout too loudly to be heard through the sound-deadening rain and mist. "Well, what did she have to say to you then?" he asked, his expression knowing.

He meant Hortense, of course. And it was the fact of his knowing, or at least his attitude of being able to give a pretty certain guess, that irrevocably and immediately erased any plans she might have had to try and dupe him. "What do you think?" she asked, able to give him a sudden, impish grin.

He groaned. "Marriage, of course. To Miss Yardley, no doubt."

She nodded.

"Better tell me the whole of it, then, so I may circumnavigate any of my beloved sister's plans for me."

"It was not too complicated a plan," Mary confessed. "I was merely to 'steer' you into Miss Yardley's company, and whisper in your ear about that lady's wonderments." She grinned at him. "But you would know better than I — does Miss Yardley have any wonderments?"

He rolled his eyes, but he answered honestly, "That she does. She is, as far as I can tell, the epitome of womanly virtue and worth. She is, as my sister so assuredly knows, the very stuff that brides are made of."

"Is she pretty?" Mary asked, and if the words did not trip easily off her tongue, she disguised that neatly by reaching up to dash some of the rain from her cheeks.

"Oh, my, yes. Possibly the prettiest woman I've ever met."

"Then you should marry her," Mary said, sitting up a little more straightly in her saddle. "Only think what beautiful children you would have together."

"Hmm, that's true enough, I suppose. But wouldn't it be awful if nature should not care for the combination, and therefore made our children ugly? Can you imagine growing up, always less beautiful than your parents? No, that argument is not enough to send me off to kneel before the lady and request her hand in eternal and everlasting matrimony. You would have to do better than that. But now you shall not have to make the attempt, for I know Hortense's plan, and thusly is it already thwarted. You realize, of course, that this is the very matter of which I could not bear to write?"

"Marriage?"

"Imminent marriage. It became quite clear to me from the moment Miss Yardley was presented to me, that not only did my family have plans for me, but they had even been so vulgar as to present those same plans to the enemy!" He put a hand to his chest, as if a mortal wound had been sustained there.

"How you do protest! Wasn't it Shakespeare who said something about 'protesting too much'?" Mary asked, one eyebrow delicately raised.

"I believe he said 'the *lady* doth protest too much'. He said nothing about any gentlemen, and so it does not apply."

"I see. Well, and now that I am found out, what are we going to do about it?"

"Why, absolutely nothing."

"No, I don't think so. I think I shall certainly give this Miss Yardley the eye. I must see this paragon for myself. If she is all Hortense believes, and if she has a sense of humor—the poor dear would need it with you—then I shall still do my best to whisper in your ear and urge you into her company," Mary said, and she almost believed the confidence she heard in her own voice,

He gave her a long, slow look from the side of his eye, and when he turned his head to face her, he growled, "Traitor!"

She smiled, but the smile flickered uncertainly. "Godfrey, you know I shall not, truly, if you do not care for—"

"It's all right, Mary. In truth, I am interested to hear what you think of this young miss. I vow, she makes me feel very old. Very old indeed. Perhaps even old enough, at last, to wed."

Mary lowered her lashes to watch as she unnecessarily adjusted the reins in her gloved hands, and it seemed suddenly to be raining harder than ever. "I think we should go back," she said toward the horse's ears.

Godfrey gave a grunt for an answer, and they turned their horses at once.

He only said one more thing as they rode along. "This home of mine, Mary, it is the strangest place. I'll confess I love it, much as one loves a leg or an arm. To be cut off from it, I should feel its loss deeply, and yet, too, it does not seem to quite fit me. I should like to be comfortable here. I should like to make it a home."

He said no more, but she filled in the rest of the words for him: he was thinking of taking a wife, that he might at last become truly the master of this place. There was some kind of invisible marker that kept him from being in possession of his own estate, that allowed his sisters and mother to exert a kind of dominance over him, and that marker could never be put aside until he had succumbed to its singular demand:

domesticity. Not until the heir had an heir would he have the kind of peace and freedom that he desired.

So it was a paradox: that he must give up his freedom to gain it.

And it was just like Godfrey to resist the commonplace, the expected, the natural flow of everyday life, even though, as she had come to see and accept, it was what he craved most in this world. Hortense was correct in this, Mary saw suddenly quite clearly, and so she knew, for once, Godfrey could not call the tune, but must instead dance to whatever tune the piper chose. Of course, it need not be Miss Yardley, and indeed *should* not be her unless the lady was, indeed, a wonderment. Nothing less would do for her dearest Godfrey, absolutely nothing less than a wonderment.

Returned to the stables, he placed his hands on her waist and helped her slide to the ground, where she lingered there before him a moment, looking up into his eyes. "It is not wrong to want to be happy," she told him. She blinked a few times, suddenly struggling against the hint of tears that came at the faintly surprised and unusually somber expression on his face. She then stepped quickly away from him, able only to quickly mumble, "Thank you for the ride." Pulling at her gloves, she moved to leave the stables and step back to the house, but he called after her, causing her to pause with her back to him.

"Mary? Will you ride tomorrow morning?"

She hesitated a moment, then nodded. She did not linger a moment longer, all but running across the rain-soaked lawn.

Chapter Ten

The ladies were on their best behavior. They sat decorously sipping tea, taking turns at speaking, laughing softly only, their conversation so dotted with 'how nice' and 'lovely' that Mary herself had difficulty with her composure. She had swiftly become accustomed to the unbridled gaiety of the Rothayne household, and though she could never fault the ladies by saying they pointed or yawned or in any other wise acted with poor manners, to see them now playing the parts of high society matrons was almost too amusing.

It was, of course, all strictly for Miss Yardley's benefit. That lady may have enjoyed the camaraderie of a usual Rothayne meal, but Hortense was not prepared to frighten her away if she was not of that ilk. No (it had been strictly adjured), the Rothayne ladies were to conduct themselves as if royalty had been asked to their little card party. Mary thought this wise, for much as she had come to enjoy Godfrey's family, and as much as she would have forgiven them much for his sake, she had to admit that she had been heartily overwhelmed and not a little shocked at first herself.

Though soon her amusement at the tempering of

the ladies' more natural tendencies was balanced by the sobering she felt whenever she glanced in Miss Yardley's direction, which, of course, must be frequently. She had been no less than stunned when the dark-haired beauty had swept into the room. It was not enough that Miss Yardley had a bounty of thick, rich (and, Mary thought in pique even as one hand reached up to push back a stray lock of her own unruly hair), *obediently in place* deepest black hair, but her milky white, sweet heart-shaped face was dominated by large dark eyes, framed by thick, sable lashes. Her cheekbones were high, her perfect lips a natural pink, her figure was slender but graced with womanly attributes, and she moved with the grace of a deer.

There was only one flaw that Mary could ascertain, her sharp eyes and ears taking in the fact with a completely unChristian lack of charity for which she immediately chided herself. She saw that Miss Yardley was quite willing and able to discuss French fashions or appropriate riding ensembles with any of the ladies, but that she colored and stammered mostly monosyllables when addressed by any of the gentlemen. *That* was a major minus to her suitability for Godfrey, for he surely would not abide a female who could not converse, Mary thought, raising one fingernail at which she absentmindedly nibbled until she hastily recalled herself and ceased at once.

However, the defect, such as it was, went through a miraculous transformation when Godfrey entered the room. Where he had been until now, Mary could only guess—hiding was a likely choice. His late entrance served to bring every eye his way, not least of those being Miss Yardley's.

"Your grace," she breathed, and to Mary's astonishment she saw the young lady rise to her feet, that face suddenly shining and ethereal in its beauty. She stood alone, the other ladies retaining their seats, and the gesture could only serve to bring Godfrey to her side at once, for he was above all else a gentleman, incapable of snubbing or discomforting a guest in his home. He took up Miss Yardley's hand and brushed the air above it with his lips, and said in greeting, "How pleasant that you could come, Miss Yardley."

Was there unusual warmth in that greeting?

"Your grace, it is my very great pleasure to be invited," Miss Yardley said.

Only a stone statue could have misunderstood the admiration in her eyes, and Godfrey was hardly a stone. Did he hold her hand just a little longer than was necessary?

"Our others guests have begun to arrive," Godfrey told the room at large.

The butler began to introduce the arriving guests, and it was nearly an hour before Godfrey was able to suggest that they begin to assemble their tables.

It was hardly surprising that Lady Rothayne assigned Miss Yardley as Godfrey's partner. Mary was at first pleased to also be assigned to the same table. She could so much more easily assess this Miss Yardley if she was in a position to interact with her, although after a certain length of time she rather wished she had not been required to observe that lady's overt — yet curiously naive — flirtation attempts. Or perhaps she was being unkind, or too harsh, for indeed Miss Yardley never said a word out of place, even if she engaged in a much more lively conversation with her eyes.

"You play whist very well," Godfrey complimented

her once.

"I do so enjoy games," she had replied, and there was such promise in the way it was said that Mary allowed a few of her cards to fall to the floor to give herself a chance to cover her own embarrassment. Sweet heavens, had Hortense primed the girl? Had she told her that Godfrey was one to enjoy a woman with spice? A quick glance at her partner convinced her otherwise, for although Hortense looked pleased, she also had a mildly startled look about her. Since Godfrey—perhaps fortuitously, perhaps not—then excused himself to fetch them all a glass of wine, Hortense took the opportunity to stand and stretch and with speaking eyes persuaded Mary to do the same. She came close to Mary's side, acting as though she had stumbled a little on the carpet, and publicly uttered an apology for her lack of balance, while she also managed to whisper quickly, "You see what I mean!"

Mary looked over her shoulder at the exquisite girl. Her smile came automatically when Miss Yardley smiled so very attractively and innocently in return, and Mary thought to herself: *Hortense is right again. This is a child waiting to know who and what she is. She speaks with her eyes, and yet I would swear she comprehends only a portion of what she so unwittingly conveys.*

Godfrey could mold Miss Yardley anyway he wanted. He, the dark angel; she, the innocent one. He could have that rare and specific being—a good woman who was capable of being tempted by the sins of the flesh, yet not dissolute. Unlike other women who tended to have their feet either on one side of that line or the other, she could be taught to walk the line, to tread on the border. That she flirted so outrageously, then offered a most sincere and sweet smile, was proof enough for Mary.

When Mary sat down again, she allowed herself to sip the entire glass of champagne that Godfrey placed before her, and even let herself have another.

Mary's table finished their game first, and they turned good-naturedly to watch the play of the others until they, too, had reached resolution. There were ten tables in all, making the guests' number twenty-six against the Rothaynes' fourteen.

"Will those of the losing teams please raise their hands?" Godfrey suggested, and he was obliged. "There is a penalty," he said after assessing who was who. "The losers must perform somehow for the winners."

"Unfair!" Harry protested. "That wasn't part of the original bargain."

"There was no bargain at all," Godfrey agreed in good humor, adding, "so the penalty stands. I suggest Mary go first, as she, I can assure you, will delight us all with her talent."

He turned to her, and, as usual, she could not deny him. "There is no harp," she said, but it was not a refusal by any means.

"A capella, then, my sweet. Your voice is true. Or perhaps Hortense can pay *her* penalty by playing the harpsichord for you?"

So it was arranged. Hortense found the sheet music for "Scarborough Fair," and Mary agreed to sing it. Harry was persuaded to play the mandolin to accompany them, and thereby pay his penalty as well. It took him a few minutes to bring the instrument from the music room, and then to tune it, and a few grumbles about it not being nearly so fine as his own at home, and then they began.

Mary made a point of singing to a particular corner of the room, for somehow she felt a little strange singing a love ballad in front of all these strangers, and besides she was just a little tipsy from the champagne, and staring at the corner served to steady her.

She fancied the applause was a little more than mere politeness when they were finished, and she thanked them for it by offering a curtsy.

Angela was then pressed into reciting a poem, "The Wreck of the Mary McGregor", as she claimed she could not sing. Aaron agreed to play the harpsichord quietly as background music, and all agreed the combination made for a lovely, if sad, recital.

This was followed by a foursome who blended their voices in a silly ditty currently all the rage at the theatres. Penelope, Sophronia, Harry, and Lady Rothayne then came together, deciding to perform a few "imitations of famous moments in history," and before long their penalty had dissolved into a full-fledged game in which all were involved. Godfrey swore his "Duke of Wellington Defeating Napoleon" was a masterpiece in the art of mime, but since no one had even come close to guessing it, he was generally booed and forced to sit down, which he did while bowing with good humor. It did not truly surprise, or even shock Mary when Miss Yardley did "Aphrodite Rising From the Sea". If that young lady knew of the famous painting, then she also surely knew that Aphrodite was without benefit of clothing, but, thankfully, she did not demonstrate such. She did, however, color prettily when Edmund pointed out that "mythology was not history, per se," which resulted in a lively exchange of opinions on the matter, which was never actually settled as they fell to laughing and going off on side tangents all

129

willy-nilly.

It was not until the candles in the front chandelier had more than half melted away that the guests finally retrieved their cloaks and gave their farewells. Miss Yardley, perhaps emboldened by the many glasses of champagne that had been served all evening long, actually reached out and took up Godfrey's hands in her own. "Thank you so much for a lovely evening," she said, her dark eyes shining with sincere appreciation and perhaps something more.

"It was our pleasure," he replied, and Mary could not help but note with approval the evenness of his tone. It was a very noncommittal tone, although she also noted that he did not extract his hands at once from Miss Yardley's tiny ones.

"I hope we may do it again sometime."

"But of course."

With that the guests were gone and the family faded back into the various sitting rooms, and Mary found herself alone in the foyer with Godfrey. He did not move for a long time, but when he did, it was to clasp his hands behind his back and turn an inquiring look her way.

"She is beautiful," Mary said, by way of a reply to his unspoken question. "And she is very young. A little gauche, perhaps, but I find I cannot dislike her."

Godfrey merely gazed at her for a minute longer, then he turned, offering her his arm. All he said was, "Quite." He escorted her to the base of the stairs, where her hand went to the carved newel in preparation of ascending. He said, "Can I not persuade you to stay belowstairs a while longer? We could . . . oh, I don't know . . . ah yes, I have it! We could strip off all our clothes and wander about together, observing the servants reactions to such. What do you say?"

She smiled, and almost reached out a hand to touch his jawline where the faintest hint of color threatened to grow into an auburn beard if given half a chance, but she did not. "Ask me again in the summertime, when it's warmer," she said with quiet humor.

How strange it was, this teasing way they had of speaking truths silently to one another. He obviously knew she had just given her approval of the young Miss Yardley as a matrimonial prospect, and she knew that he was thinking, most weightily, along those very same lines. But she could not let him go without letting him know she had still some small measure of reserve concerning Miss Yardley. "Perhaps you should ask Miss Yardley if she might be interested in such a proposal."

His eyes widened a little, then changed into a hooded expression. "What would she say?" he murmured.

"That, my dear, is the crux," she said, almost whispering.

He lifted a hand, giving her a silent 'good night,' and stepped back from her. She turned and stepped with outward calm up the stairs, but in her heart a hundred tiny storms waged battle one upon the other. She had seen Miss Yardley tonguetied with the gentlemen, though she had come to life when Godfrey had entered the room. What did it mean? Did it mean that she would have the conversation, the wit, that Godfrey required as some men required their pints of ale? Beauty could please the eye, could even warm the soul, but it could not touch the heart. And Godfrey's heart had not been sculpted for

131

anything less than love.

And she, Mary, silently, secretly, admitted for the merest of seconds to herself that perhaps *she* possessed the one thing Miss Yardley did not: this understanding, this meeting of minds, this facility, born of both words and of silence, this conversational way between she and Godfrey. And as much as she wished Godfrey to find his perfect mate, and as much as she knew it was selfish and thoughtless of her, there was a darker side of her that strongly, almost violently, hoped that Miss Yardley did *not* possess it, ever. This talent was, after all, quite possibly Mary's only redeeming attribute as a desirable female, and she found she had the ability to desire fiercely that it not be shared by the practically perfect Miss Yardley.

Chapter Eleven

To Mary's surprise, and not a little regret, the week sped by swiftly. There were two more occasions, tea parties, whereby she was in the presence of the undeniably fine Miss Yardley. That lady managed to be the center of all activity, which of course must be expected of a guest, even if Mary found herself somewhat militantly thinking that she, too, was a guest. But that was unfair, for Miss Yardley had the grace and charm and beauty that must needs draw the eye and the attention of anyone. Even, Mary grudgingly admitted, herself.

But if she spent her afternoons thoughtfully weighing the virtues of Miss Yardley, she spent her mornings blissfully riding with the Rothayne gentlemen. There she was queen, for even though some of the ladies had bothered themselves once or twice to rise and join the pack, they soon tired of the rain, and besides, Mary knew it was *her* presence which was truly appreciated. She knew that the gents looked forward to the repartee that was nearly as essential a part of the ride as were the horses themselves. Everyone, their minds cleared of clutter by a night's sleep, excelled at clever quips and witticisms, or even biting political commentary, so that they chortled and applauded as a group their own cleverness. It was an entirely hedonistic time, for the gentlemen had become used to speaking their minds before her, and Mary revelled in the camaraderie and acceptance it meant even if it was, if one chose to look at it that way, not entirely complimentary to her femininity.

"I say, I am of a mind that Eugenia is with child again," Harry announced this last morning of Mary's stay. He did not blush, nor stammer, nor apologize for the statement before Mary, nor did she color up in the slightest.

"Another girl, no doubt," Godfrey said drolly, while guiding his horse around a suspicious bit of muddy ground that might be turned up as a result of a gopher's work.

"I suspect as much. But it doesn't stand to reason, does it?" Harry replied. "There are such things as *odds,* you know."

"All stacked against us," Aaron put in.

"Well, perhaps I am jumping the gun. Eugenia has said nothing to me."

They looked at one another, then shook their heads, and agreed that Harry probably had the right of it.

"And what of you, Aaron? When are you going to produce some offspring? Perhaps your new blood will run true?" Timothy asked, not sparing the young man his blushes, for he was young and unable yet to make light of life's more serious endeavors.

"Newly married, old chap," Aaron mumbled into his cravat.

The others had a chuckle at his expense, but then Edmund said, "Besides, it's not Aaron that our wives

134

drive us mad about, Timothy. It's Godfrey, of course."

"Really?" Godfrey asked blankly, as though in complete innocence. "Do you mean to say that my breeding capabilities are a part of your pillow talk?"

Edmund refused to rise to the bait. "Quite right," he said, every bit as droll as Godfrey. "And I for one grow quite weary of it. 'Godfrey this,' and 'Godfrey that. Will he marry. When will he marry? Whom shall he marry?' I vow you have no care for us other poor souls, for you do nothing to relieve us of this burden."

"You are suggesting that I tell my sisters they are not to make a sound once you are abed? I could do so, if you truly so desire."

"Edmund, it's no use. The man's as callous as the bottom of a savage's foot," Harry said, laughing in quiet amusement. "If these women of ours could not make him marry 'fore now, there is no hope that we could ever persuade him to do so."

"At last we are speaking sensibly!" Godfrey said approvingly.

"But what of Miss Yardley?" Aaron chimed in, his blushes at last receding, only to be born anew under Godfrey's cool sideways glare. "I mean, it seems to me . . . that is . . .," he stammered.

"Let us speak instead of Lady Mary," Godfrey said, turning to her so that she saw the light of displeasure that still lingered in his eyes. "I must inform you all that she is being so cruel as to abandon us this day, my fellows."

"Already?"

"Never say it's so!"

"Stay another week, at least."

Mary felt an aching warmth grow inside her, a

combination of thankfulness for their sincere regret mingled with her own. Nonetheless, she knew, via Mrs. Pennett's eye on the calendar if not her own logic, it was surely time to go, and so she said lamely, "I must get back to London."

"By Jove, I've a thought!" Timothy announced suddenly. "I've got business waiting for me in London as well. I had planned to stay another day or so here, but since you must travel now, why don't I just change my plans and go along with you? It would save Godfrey's horses a return trip," he explained. "Angela can return with Hortense."

"Of course," Mary said, smiling in his direction, but it was really Godfrey that she watched from the corner of her eye, because for a moment she had seen him frown. A second later a noncommittal look had settled across his features. She knew full well, perhaps better than even those of his family, that this meant he was not quite pleased. But of course he was not, for he himself longed to return to town, and he must be feeling just a trifle jealous of Lord Gateway's freedom to leave.

And so it was that Timothy's bags were added to the top of her father's carriage as soon as the luncheon was over. Angela presented him with a list of things to do and purchases to make before she returned home to London, a week hence, and gave him an earful of verbal instructions as well. Their daughters, Katherine and Suzanne, each gave their father a hug, and extracted a promise for a surprise of some kind when they were reunited. Hortense requested that Timothy send a note 'round to her staff, to inform them that she would be returning to London soon.

Mary looked on, unable to suppress the small sigh

of covetousness that passed her lips as she observed the cozy familial scene. Well, she had not been gone from London long, and so she had every hope that there was still enough season left for her to fulfill her plans of matrimony, and subsequently this burning desire for a family of her own.

"You are sad to leave me," Godfrey put his interpretation on the sigh. He stood at her side, just outside the front foyer.

"I am. But there is much work yet to be done in London, and Mother is expecting my return."

"I will be coming soon, my pet," he said, taking her hand and pressing it to his lips. It was not the formal kiss of a stranger, but rather a caress of his lips in truth against the back of her fingers. She did her best to suppress the quiver that ran suddenly and unexpectedly through her, and all but snatched her hand from his, pretending to need it to gather up the basket of goodies that the Rothayne chef had assembled for the travelers.

"Perhaps I shall be engaged before you ever return to London," she said in a manner she could only define as 'gabbling' as she strode purposefully toward the open door of the carriage.

"Let me wish you good hunting then," Godfrey said, offering her a hand up the steps.

She shook her head in mild vexation with him, for it had not sounded much like a joke to her. His words had carried a bit of the infamous 'Blade' sarcasm in them. "Thank you," she said somewhat drily as she settled on the squabs of the carriage, looking out at him with less than completely sincere eyes.

"Mary," he said, then hesitated. "Forgive me. I am not quite myself. This country life — it turns me swiftly into a clod."

"Then spend more time with your steward and be done with your work here!" she chided him, but she had softened yet again toward him at this, his rare act of offering an apology.

"I will, for my Mary has said I must." He smiled at her, and at last she could smile back.

"And don't spend too much time with Miss Yardley, or else you may never escape here," she dared to tease.

Fortunately the quip succeeded, for he laughed and agreed that it was sound advice. "Let me tell you, I am wondering what the creature has to say for herself, for we never really have had a chance to chat. Now that I am desperate yet again for companionship, I shall avail myself of her time as to at last arrange the possibility of knowing."

"She's a beauty," Mary said on a sigh, for there was no denying that which was truth.

Of form, there can be no doubt. I'll write. Better yet, I'll finish my work, and come to you. Soon. I have vested interests in whomsoever shall be your groom, and would like to inspect him thoroughly before you are wed, for my own peace of mind."

"Do that."

"Farewell. Don't let Gateway talk your ear off. If he so much as mentions his interest in pulleys, you are to kindly but firmly cut him off at once."

"I'll remember that. Godfrey, take care."

"I shall. Godspeed, Mary."

She smiled warmly, if a little sadly, for she had spent her morning saying farewell to the large hosting body that had entertained and appreciated her this week past, and—truth be told—she did not really want to leave them, though she must for the sake of inner peace. It had been a warm and welcoming interlude, but, too, it had been disturbing at times.

Godfrey's strong hand reached into the carriage, took her arm and pulled her toward him a little. He did not kiss her cheek, as she was half prepared for, but instead kissed her full on the lips. She knew nothing else for a moment but the feel of his mouth on hers, and could not help the fact that she kissed him back.

He did not release her hand, so that she had to sit back and pull it from his grip. Their eyes met, and for a moment she allowed a spark to flare between them.

"Good heavens, Godfrey! Have a care for your rag-tattered manners," Hortense scolded.

Mary's lids lowered over her betraying eyes, for she had seen that Hortense's words had brought a wolf-ish grin to his lips, and she could not bear to think he might see that she was unable to take the kiss lightly, even as he obviously did.

Timothy apparently saw nothing wrong with the exchange, for he chatted easily, "This is a fine carriage, Mary. I can only respect your father's choice in both his comforts and his horseflesh. That's a fine pair of goers you brought down with you."

Mrs. Pennett gazed across the carriage interior at her charge, but her face was as carefully blank as Mary's.

"Thank you," Mary said absently as the carriage door was closed. She allowed one huge ripple to course through her, but then she rallied and turned to the window to offer a small wave. Godfrey lifted his hand in a single salute, and then the carriage turned in the drive and she could no longer see him.

"What was that Godfrey was saying about pulleys? Did he happen to mention that I have made quite a study of a variety of pulley systems . . .?"

She let him talk on, let him fill her head with incomprehensible facts and supposed points of interest, let him distract her heart, to prevent that poor organ from fulfilling its one true wish to slump down into her boots for a good old-fashioned sulk.

Chapter Twelve

Godfrey walked the field next to his steward, pausing occasionally to bend down and feel the soil with his hands, or to nudge a clod of dislodged grass back into place. He made a concerted effort to hear what the man was saying, but it was in truth not much more than a repeated recitation of the reasons why he could not return to London just yet.

"The vet'nary, 'e's comin' up tamorra ta 'ave a look at them cattle agin," the steward, James Rigger, said seriously. "I 'ope that whae'er 'is diagnosis, that ta cattle kin go ta market. It's comin' up soon, yer knows, ta market . . ."

But try as he might, Godfrey found his attention straying. One minute he was listening, and the next he was caught up in the diversion of watching a flight of swallows overhead, or a mare running in the adjoining pasture, or thoughts of the conversation at table last night, or wispy, unfocused remembrances from days both recent and long past.

He recalled such a day as this, cool, crisp, with breaks in the fat white clouds. The clouds, then as now, were whisked about high in the atmosphere by a wind that did not deign to touch the earth, causing the clouds and the sun to play a game of hide and seek far above the heads of the mortals below. So it had been on that other day, the day that his heart had first been touched with the frost of unrequited love. Melinda. Pretty, clever, cruel Melinda. Although the thought of her no longer caused that organ which resided in his chest to contract painfully, still the thought of her was a sobering one, and unwelcome. Especially unwelcome today, for some reason he could not even begin to imagine. He forced his mind back to the conversation at hand, until yet again the steward's words began to pale, leading his thoughts once again astray. It was time to move on, then, if he could not concentrate, so he bid his steward good day, and realized that this move only left him two options: he could visit Miss Yardley, as he had promised he would do sometime today, or he could stay locked in his own thoughts the rest of this not altogether comfortable nor pleasant day. He chose the former.

Still, the ruse proved no defense when he found himself alone. Free to be totally distracted, Godfrey gave up the fight and allowed his mind to wander where it would as he drove. The lane was wide and even, his nag was content, and the dogcart was a simple vehicle that did not require much of his attention. He had deliberately chosen the dogcart, for it did not have room for more than one other person. If Miss Yardley wished to ride with him, it would be without benefit of a companion.

The thought of a companion made him smile just a little, for a picture of Mrs. Pennett leaped into his mind. She had given a little taste of her spirit, that spirit so dedicated to her darling Mary, and it had surprised him at the time. He had been playing cards, not even seated at table with Mrs. Pennett's charge, and yet he had looked up to see that lady, stitching as usual in the corner, giving him the most serious look he had ever been given. At his returned scrutiny, she did not blink, nor in any wise back down, and he had the uncanny feeling that she was telling him something. Ah well, that then was easy enough to decipher, with a reputation such as his: "stay away from my girl," of course. And yet, too, it had been something more . . . but what? *That* was the puzzlement. For had he read some deeply buried, yet nonetheless real, hint of *approval* there? It was a contradiction. He must stay away and yet she liked him . . . but it couldn't be both at once! If one wanted to be rid of another's presence, one could not, surely, also like them . . . ?

For one of the rare moments since he had left his innocence behind, Godfrey did not understand what ought to have been eminently understandable. That is what made him smile now, for Mary's advent into his life had had that same effect on everything.

He had had no intention of respecting his family's wishes, but suddenly Mary was there, telling him that, yes, he ought to marry, and now he found himself mulling over the very idea that a week ago he would have sworn he should never care to give so much as a thought. Where once he would have let his mother prattle on about such silliness without so much as a peep of annoyance from himself, just this week he had roared at her that he had heard quite enough, and all, in truth, because he found the topic had somehow become embarrassing just because Mary sat at his table. The gaucheness of his family had mortified him, until he saw the upturned corners of sweet Mary's mouth. The loveliness of his estate had never struck him as such a point of pride until he saw the approving glitter in Mary's soft brown eyes. All the old pains of returning to this place, the home of his youthful follies, had been as nothing as soon as the good lady had placed one tiny slippered foot upon its soil. It was her musical laughter, and the lilting sound of her voice raised in those ancient songs of love and adoration that came so pleasingly from her lips, not to mention the comfortable silences that they had shared, that now filled his ears.

Too, there had been a moment other than these — a moment that had rocked him for the time it lasted. It had started so simply: he had only meant to give her a brief, salutary kiss. A kiss to send her safely on her way. Somewhere, somehow, even in its brevity, it had become much more than that: he had seen without a doubt that Mary was a being waiting for love. She thought her only desire was for children, that everything else could be put aside in the pursuit of such, but he had seen her more clearly. That kiss, so revealing, had shown him just a hint of the passionate nature that no one knew existed within the lady.

The knowledge was vitally important. He knew now, more than ever before, that not just any fellow would do for Mary. The lucky man must be capable of affection, must be able to fall in love with her. It meant that he, Godfrey, must look all the harder at the applicants to that position, for even Mary herself did not really know what she must have, what sort of person her husband must be if she was to go on being his dearest, most extraordinary Mary.

Ah, Mary, my heart, he sighed to himself, *how I miss you already and only one day gone. How did you slip past my defenses so cleanly and easily? Why did I let you open my eyes again to the innocence, and the complications, of life simply lived?*

144

And there were still too many days to go before he could return to London. Just this morning hadn't his steward been again telling him of the sale of the Jordan property at auction? It was not adjacent to, but very near his own. He would be a fool to let some other landowner purchase it. Such an investment might recoup, not this year, but next, some of their losses, and would in any event be good land to own. And there was that danger of disease with the cattle to consider. There were the formal documents to be signed, if those cattle were allowed to go to market. Not to mention the new roofs he had ordered on three of the estate cottages, and that blasted stone fence that had been discovered could not be rebuilt in the same place, for fear of the same thing happening later . . . all of which could be handled by his steward, if only Georgette had not developed a fever. It was not uncommon, said the doctor, following birth, but Godfrey could not, and would not, leave until she was recovered. Mama was quite beside herself with concern. There was no hope of leaving for London soon, so as a diversion for himself he had thought to write to the Yardleys to see if he might pay a visit. His inquiry had been immediately answered, to the affirmative.

As he moved toward that engagement, Godfrey's mind slid past thoughts and impressions of the lovely Miss Yardley, aimlessly to thoughts of how he would have asked Mary along this day, to come with him to review the same. He would have asked Mary the best way to learn more of this young creature, how to bring out her true opinions, for he knew full well that the ladies of his circle oft times said what they ought, not what they thought. And in truth, he would have used Mary as a kind of buffer, a way to keep the ardent-eyed Miss Yardley from being too forward.

That thought made him laugh aloud, for it was not usually his way to wish a beautiful woman *out* of his arms, but—he thought more soberly—this was not a matron with full knowledge of her deeds; this was a "marriageable," with certain expectations, and thereby entailed with certain consequences to certain actions. Women had one set of rules; young misses another. And Miss Annalee Yardley was a young miss, make no mistake.

He sighed then, and was almost glad to see the clouds once again closing over the brief bit of sun that had begun his journey. Had he wanted to persuade Miss Yardley to drive alone with him? No, he could not really fool himself, and knew it had never been his intention. The imminent rain only served to make it that much less likely.

He noted how the front doors were pulled open for him in a manner more styled for royalty, and how the daughter, mother, and father of the house stood just inside the door to greet him the very second his boot first touched their flooring. His hat and coat were solicited, and then his need for drink, followed by edible refreshments. Only when he had denied the latter two did the threesome recall themselves enough to let their guest step aside that the doors might be closed. He was then offered profuse apologies for the lapse, followed by an escort into the front parlor, where once again he was offered a round of refreshments, which he decided to accept as it seemed so very important to them.

A heavily loaded teatray explained at a glance that their cook had been hard pressed to produce a number of wonders, not least of which was a spun-sugar bowl of tiny marzipan fruits, nearly hidden as it was among the tea cakes, trimmed sandwiches, fresh fruit tarts, sugared nuts, variety of sweetmeats, and cleverly carved slices of ham and cheese that he took to be representations of the Yardley coat of arms.

Having lunched just before he came, he found the display a bit overwhelming . . . and not just the edibles; also the daughter. Miss Yardley was dressed in the very latest frock, cut daringly low for a day dress, with gossamer fabrics that hinted at the charming form beneath. Godfrey found himself a trifle disconcerted that parents should allow such an ensemble, at least in the full light of day, and also for the blatant display of consent it so obviously implied. He found himself thinking that he could very well have that ride alone in the dogcart with Miss Yardley, if he were to so much as open his mouth and mention the idea.

He vowed in a moment's time that if Lord Yardley asked to speak a moment with him, that he would at once have to develop a tremendous headache, or some such by which to refuse such a meeting, for he could see that they had every hope and expectation of an offer for their daughter's hand. It couldn't be more clear than if they had hung a sign about her neck which read "take me, please".

He accepted a cup of tea, trying to murmur small appropriate noises when he must, for his mind kept trying to slide far away from anything resembling attention to the conversation.

It was not that he had no idea of how to undo their hopes—that was a simple thing, in fact. He was practiced at dashing presumptions. No, it was instead the unusual inability to decide if that was really what he wanted to do or not. They wanted him—did

147

he want the girl? He turned his sea-sky gaze to the daughter of the house, and was rewarded by a bright, yes, even stunning, smile. It was an eager smile, one that promised much. And she was too young to promise those things in falsehood, of that he would swear. She was not capable of complicated games, as were others from his past. Even so little as a few years ago, he would have been deeply cautious, but experience had proved him not completely incapable of assessing other people, so that now he felt some confidence in his conclusions. Should he rethink his first impulse to run and hide, allow himself to be open to the occasion? Mary had told him yes, and Mary cared for him. She would not lead him into harm's way, of that, too, he could swear. No, that he *knew*.

He settled back in the chair they had offered him, and feeling rather uncharacteristically awkward and not some little bit clownish, allowed them to paint a pretty, perfect, pastoral scene around him with their barely veiled hints at a connection. And though he was nobody's fool, and could rightly call himself an intelligent man, all the while he wished Mary were here, for that sense of not quite understanding overcame him again, and he longed for her to explain it all to him.

Chapter Thirteen

Mary found that she was able to slide easily back into the world of parties and fetes, dances and musicales. Her absence had only served to make her more popular, as her brief sojourn meant she might have something new and interesting to say. And so she did, though she was careful to tell no tales on her hosts, for that would have been unseemly, and also served to stir up longings to return there. And how easily she had forgotten London's propriety! She chafed a little under the daily censure, the gossip that told all, that made one watch one's tongue, but at the same time she welcomed it, for it kept her mind very busy, this routine of thrust and parry, come and go, take but not give, or at least give only a little in return.

She had gone sailing with Lord Spafford, but that had proved to be a sad event. She had been forced to dedicate nearly all her time to poor Mrs. Pennett, who alternately laid upon a bunk with a cool cloth to her head, or felt the need to hurry above "for air". Mary did not know if seasickness was contagious, but after a while she had not felt so well herself, and firmly made up her mind that she was never sailing again, and so she knew she must discount Lord Spafford as a groom-to-be.

Lieutenant Hargood had returned to London, and made a point of securing at least one dance from her whenever they met. She enjoyed his ability to move gracefully, and so often gave him two dances. If this occasioned some whispered speculations, well, that was all right, too. Lieutenant Hargood was a man with an ear for talk, and to hear of himself would not displease him; it might even steer him the sooner in the direction of more serious contemplations, Mary believed. She could not much care for the thought of being a military wife, having to move about, and she did not think the Lieutenant terribly well-to-do, but (as she told herself) "beggars can't be choosers". He was serious-minded, well-read, a fine dancer, and reasonably attractive. A woman could do much worse, Mary assured herself.

Lord Faver still sought her out for dances, as well, but he had a knack of wanting to talk softly through the exercise, causing Mary to have to often ask him to repeat himself. She amused herself with thoughts of a sort of verbal duel taking place, as they came together, called something quickly, came away, and back together for a reply or a call of "what was that?" Yet, when the dance was finished, and they were moved to the side of the room, he seemed to lose most of his ability to speak, only instead nodding or shaking his head and murmuring 'hmmm-mmm' in time to her comments. Although his reticence did not unduly upset her, she did find herself wondering if he would be able to speak at all were they to find themselves alone together.

Of her suitors, if such they could be called, it was Mr. Bretwyn who seemed the most likely to possess both the ability to speak a proposal, as well as to initiate one. He was a fine fellow, with a bright mind, an ability to tell a tale or two, and a ready smile. Mary thought well of him, for it was clear he would be the kind to watch over the family fortunes rather than spend them; to have affections in this life, if not any grand passions; and to settle comfortably to the ways and works of a wedded pair. His only acute flaw was that he favored a pipe, but Mary knew such women as forbade them in their homes, and she suspected Charles would not mind having an excuse to stroll to his club of an evening were she to follow their example. Yes, he had all these attributes, plus the reassuring one of seeking out her company deliberately. His sister, Letitia, had never again shown so overtly her interests in that direction, but Mary knew, if she were to ask outright, what Letitia's advice and wishes would be.

It was therefore disheartening to find that she had no real enthusiasm in the playing of the game, and only wished time away, so that she could have already been given and accepted an offer. But it was early days yet, for all that Mary felt this way, and she knew she could not rush her fences.

It was in a rather melancholy frame of mind that she found herself at a Hazard Party at Lord Faver's. The play had not gone her way, and therefore in no way lightened the day. She had excused herself from the table and gone in search of punch for lack of anything more inspiring to do. Mrs. Pennett was not to be seen, and so was probably at the lady's necessary, as she was nothing if she was not punctilious about attending her charge. Taking up a glass of punch, Mary decided to wander about until such time as Mrs. Pennett made her reappearance, and then she thought she might return home, the evening having been less than sparkling. There was no dancing, and Lord Spafford had avoided her ever since she had had the bad grace to have a seasick companion, and Lieutenant Hargood was gone on duty again. Lord Faver was busy entertaining his guests, and the Bretwyns were not in attendance. Mary had already circled and greeted the others she knew, and did not relish the thought of doing so again. It was natural then, surely, that her mind returned to the letter from Godfrey she had received just today.

It had started with its usual protestations against his family, except for a happy point that told her Georgette was much on the mend. Then came a couple of bittersweet references to "your abandonment of me to my fate," but then the tone had changed:

*Ah, Mary, I find myself thinking of you and my eldest protagonist (I mean Hortense, not Mother), closeted together so many times. I shudder to think what she must have told you of me! I was a beastly child, I feel sure—*Mary had shaken her head, for she had never heard anything but what a delightful child he had been to his many sisters—*but an even more beastly man. I feel somehow compelled to defend myself, to tell my side of the story, in my own way and words. Will you indulge me? If not—for nothing is more boring than when a man writes of himself—then you have but to burn this. But pray do not return the ashes to me, for I find I do not care to truly know if you have read these words or not. Foolish, I know, but you already knew this of me, and loved me anyway.*

What to say, now that I am down to it? What did Hortense whisper in your ear? Ah well, of my 'sup-

posed broken heart', no doubt. And truth, dearest, is that she is right, in a way. I did break my heart. However, fifteen years hence I have sewn it back together rather well, well enough that I do not look upon Miss Yardley with all-consuming terror, as once I might have done.

And so the tale begins: I was a young lad. Twenty. An age of stupidity, all told. Aye, and even so for women, not just men. For this is the age when a woman makes choices, sometimes based on nothing more than a notion, or as pathetic a thing as how one appears on the surface.

Her name was Melinda. That is enough of a name by which to call her, as she is married now. She was fair, light and lovely. In truth, I do not remember her face well now, but do not think me too peculiar when I say that I do recall she had lovely, even, white teeth. Such a smile! Radiant enough that it is what I retain of her now. As to her nose or eyes or mouth, perhaps I would know them if I saw them, but I do not recall them, and neither do I try to do so. Perhaps I remember those teeth because she laughed all the time. I do not have a memory, none at all, where she is not laughing, not even at the end.

After nine weeks of acquaintance, I bid her be my wife. She told me 'yes', and—now, remember you promised to blush no more before me (or even my written words)—I tell you she said 'aye' to more than just my title. We found ourselves tumbled together, in the way, I suppose, of many young lovers. I thought such intimacies meant that we were 'one', as the ancient sayings go, and therefore did not think to question if that were so. I allowed myself to fall deeply in love with her—no, not with her, but what I thought her to be. And I allowed her murmured re-

153

marks as to my physical beauty — there speaks my vanity again! — to have the same sound to my young ears as would words of love.

Imagine my surprise when a week later we were engaged no more, and a month after that she was wed to another. I had thought, for a while, this was some kind of test or game, but I could not believe that any longer when I sat in the church and watched her take her vows to the other fellow. Of course, my father was well and hale in those days, and it seems the lady was not willing to wait to have a title.

'Well', I told myself, 'I guess we were not meant to be.' So, although I smarted, and had grown much wiser by far, I was foolish enough to try the whole again. Sandra was as dark as Melinda had been fair. She was much the same in style though, and I think that is what caught my eye at first. Ah, but how people told us of how fine we looked together! It was quite heady, to be part of such a pair. But, no longer being a green boy, I was much more cautious this time. We were betrothed for six months, during which time I was as chaste as any priest in a remote and womanless village. I thought me that if the lady could be devoted for a length of time, it would be proof of her steadfastness.

They say that God watches over fools, and it must be true, for the day came when I was convinced of her, and she of me, and so she allowed me to know more than the touch of her lips on mine. But she had miscalculated, for though I was young and had been a long time celibate, I was no longer a complete fool. It was clear that here was no maiden.

And still, I meant to be not too judgmental, not too exacting, and thought of Melinda, and how I had not left her intact for her eventual husband. But

154

some wise voice whispered in my head, and I told the lady I must delay the wedding a while yet. She was not happy for it, and talked to me often to try and persuade me otherwise, but it was not two months later that there was no disguising the fact that she was increasing, and that it could not possibly be my child. The proof of this was come into the world four months later, a big, healthy, timely baby girl.

There then, are my tales. I am not afraid to tell you that I sought no faithfulness after that. I have slept where I was bidden, but I have never pretended to anything more than amusement. There is not a woman who could say otherwise. I've made no promises. I know you have heard rumors of my antics, and quite some few of them are true, as I have never tried to hide from you.

They say the measure of a friend is when they know you well, and love you still. I pray—again my Mary has me praying!— that you will love me still, as ever I adore you.

(I realize it is not quite the same thing, for I am wicked, and you are not, but perhaps my sad stories have moved your heart a little, and you are not quite ready to cast me off.)

Remembering the letter, and how the words— words of pain and heartache, of betrayal and trust gone awry—those things he had written between the lines of script, perhaps without even meaning to, how they had caught at her heart. He had silently pleaded for forgiveness, as if it was hers to give, but it was not. Forgiveness must come of himself, though the thought that he believed there was a thing to forgive made her eyes glisten with unshed tears for him. She understood then that to host a great beauty

155

could be as heavy a burden as to have a face that held no beauty at all.

It was then, as she stood in an alcove, staring off into space with eyes that shone with tears in the candlelight, that a shadow fell over her and caused her to slowly recall herself, and turn to see who was come to her side.

"Lady Wagnall, how very great a pleasure to see you again."

She managed a weak smile with one side of her mouth, but even that quickly faded as she replied, "Lord Stephens. You are returned."

"Ah, how you delight my heart, by telling me that you have noticed my absence," he said, catching up her hand to bow low over it.

She pulled her hand away, only grateful that he had not kissed it, and said, perhaps too harshly, "I could not help but notice it."

"Lady Wagnall, I do not know why you have taken me in such dislike," he said, and there was a note of hurt in his voice, enough to make her instantly feel regretful that she had not tried to be more subtle. But his next words erased that softer feeling, as he said, "But I assure you I am as fine a fellow as any of these that you pursue. I, too, am an aging man in need of a wife, and therefore not so particular as some. Come, we are of an age to be less coy, so I tell you honestly your shocked looks do not give my tongue the order to cease and desist. Why not be forthright? For what other purpose do you frolic here? Indeed, Lady Wagnall, put an end to all this posturing and wondering of 'who' and 'when', and take me instead. We could be wed in a week's time. That would suit us both, would it not?"

She stared at him, some part of her brain thinking

that he was as outspoken as her beloved Duke, but then, no, there was a difference between these cutting words and Godfrey's, for the one was cruel, and the other merely clever and never meant to wound.

Another shadow fell across her, and this time across the Baronet Stephens as well. It was Godfrey standing there, and Godfrey saying quietly, "You, sir, are no gentleman."

He reached out a hand, his thumb and forefinger closing in a tight pinch upon Lord Stephens' nose.

"Ouch!" cried that fellow, but as his hands would have come up to bat away the offending member, one was caught in Godfrey's own large hand. It was a moment's work to step to one side of Stephens and bring his arm up behind his back, causing the man to give another bellow of pain, his nose still held aloft by that firm grip.

"Pray give your apologies to the lady," Godfrey said calmly.

"My abologies," Lord Stephens tried to say. "Ow! Wothayne, you are hurding me!"

"Yes, quite. Now, explain to the lady that you will never offend her with your presence again."

Lord Stephens gave Godfrey a wild-eyed look, but an extra tug at his nose caused him to cry out hurriedly, "I was twying to be logical, dat's all. An old maid, an old man—Ouch! You bwute! Let go of me, I say—Ow! Aw wight, aw wight! Lady Wagdall, I will not bovver you again. Ever. I know when I'm not wanted."

"At last," Godfrey said. "Now we will go and make your excuses to our host, shall we not?"

Mary followed them from the alcove, her hands covering her mouth to hold back either laughter or sobs, she could not say which, and she watched as

Lord Stephens was escorted by his nose past Lord Faver, allowed to pause just long enough to give another holler by way of a farewell, and then he was ushered out the door. Laughter from the many observant eyes then broke out, which rolled on as the Duke returned to the room. He carefully dusted his hands together, like a man who has just carried old ashes out to the dustbin, and was heard to murmur, "It's the only way to handle some bull-headed fellows," which was followed by even more laughter.

Mary moved across the room, feeling strangely dreamlike, for it was difficult to recover one's poise after having been so roundly insulted, and then rescued. And rescued by no less than her sunkissed Godfrey. She whispered his name, and he stretched out his hands and took up both of hers within his.

"Well met, Mary. But, please, erase the dread from your eyes: the Baronet will not dare to breathe a word of what he said, for it would only lead him toward greater humiliation."

"You are returned," she said, and noted even in her bemused state how differently she reacted to the return of this man over the return of the Baronet Stephens.

"You see a free man! My steward at last can handle the business himself. My sister is recovered. And I am escaped."

"Godfrey, thank you. Thank you so much for what you just did. You do not know what a pest Lord Stephens had made of himself—"

"He'll pester you no more. But, of his words, Mary, will *they* pester you?" he asked seriously, dropping her hands as he realized others were gawking at them, at the length of time they had done nothing but stand and speak directly to one another with clasped hands between them. He crossed his arms over his chest, his expression defiant.

"Well, as to that, I'll admit they stung. I have to wonder, how many others see through my attendance here? How many others guess it is a husband, not gaiety, that I seek?"

"Everyone," he answered at once, but to take the sting out of the words he added, "That is what these gatherings are for, after all. And you have expectations, and a fine face, and a lovely way about you. No one thinks the less of you that you follow the natural course of things."

"Maybe I should forget matrimony. I could open a shop of some kind . . ." she sighed.

"And well you would do there, for you are clever, but it would not bring you children," he reminded her.

"Ah," she agreed with another sigh, only to push the glum-filled mood away by dint of a smile up at him. "Tonight serves me no such purpose then, either. My suitors are well busied or in nonattendance, unable to court me. And now I see Mrs. Pennett coming my way. I think I will persuade her that we ought to return home."

"Then I will come with you."

"No," she said, her voice low, for belatedly she, too, had become aware of the notice they had drawn.

He shook his head, as if she had struck him there, but then he was smiling naughtily, and saying, "You're right. We can't have it getting around that I've gone off with you. Might scare off the suitors."

"That, added to the fact that you saved me from Lord Stephens," she said with a heavy heart, for she hated to refuse herself his company, and she hated to deny him even so little a thing. She had never denied him anything before, no, not even the offerings of romantic moments he had claimed he wanted to indulge in with her, for that was only play. How much more disturbed would he appear if she had ever said 'yes' to any of those humorous offerings? she wondered.

"Good evening," she said, quickly laying a hand atop his folded arms, taking the hand away just as quickly as she turned to greet her companion. "Gladys, I find I am weary and wish to go home."

"Of course. Come along, we'll fetch our shawls," Mrs. Pennett agreed at once, but as she did so she looked over the top of her charge's head and gave Godfrey another one of those indecipherable looks.

He actually startled, and almost spoke, to demand that the companion explain herself, but then the ladies had turned, leaving him with his lips slightly parted in mute inquiry as they walked away, the younger of the two oblivious to his consternation with the elder.

Chapter Fourteen

"Tell me what brought you back to England," Mary said.

Godfrey glanced down at her, then back to his pair of grays, for the road was crowded this afternoon, and his attention could only be divided. "You mean after the banishment?"

"Yes."

"Nerve, I suppose. I was far away and forgotten, and had no reason to think that Prinny should be glad to see me again."

"But you dared show your face. Why?" Mary asked. She lifted a hand and nodded toward an acquaintance, but then turned her face, not wanting to stop and chat with the lady. She had Godfrey all to herself today, Mrs. Pennett notwithstanding.

He sighed, checked his horses a little to the right to avoid a heavily loaded wagon, and then answered, "England is home, of course. A man eventually longs for home. I even missed my sisters." He grinned.

She grinned back. "Then you were *truly* homesick."

"Or insane. I have not decided which."

"I for one am glad you made the decision to come home."

"Me, too," he said, but she could not exactly glow in the warmth of the admission, for it was clear his thoughts stretched on beyond her. He spoke slowly, a hint of amazement in his voice, showing again a side of the man few knew existed, this man who could be astounded by what life had shown him. "The world is full of many strange things—some are wondrous, some are terrible. And if I learned nothing else from my travels, I did at least learn that one simple fact is true no matter where you go. So why *not* home? Why not take a risk, and find out the strength and length of royal censure? If it meant there was a possibility that at last I could go where the wondrous and terrible things were at least familiar, then it was worth the attempt. And Prinny, speak as you will of him, is incapable of holding a grudge over what was truly a simple nothingness. I wrote him, telling him I wished to return to the land of my birth. Not only did he allow the thing, but he even went so far as to give me a public reception of sorts, to show I was not still completely outside his favor. S'truth, that is why I am acceptable again, why I need not rusticate in Kent as 'the shunned Duke.' I am grateful to him for giving me back what once I had lost."

Mary gazed at his serious expression, at the honest appreciation she saw there. "Then I am grateful to him also. For it was at that reception that I first met you."

Godfrey smiled softly down at her, and for a moment she thought the sun had come to live in his eyes. She was so taken by that handsome visage, that caring smile he cast upon her, that she found that her heart was thudding so deliberately in her breast that she was surprised he did not comment on it. "And you will never say another misthought word in his presence," she managed to tease breathlessly.

"Oh, I couldn't swear as to that!"

They laughed together, for it was true enough. Godfrey held his tongue for no man it seemed, not even his Regent.

When they were at their destination, he worked the horses to a place at the side of the lane, and tossing the reins to his ostler, he helped both ladies down from the carriage.

"First the lace. Everything depends on the lace," Mrs. Pennett declared. They had come to view the new fabrics just arrived from Brussels, with the hope of finding something suitable for a new dress or two for Mary. Mrs. Pennett stepped forward, leading the way toward the shopfronts, instead of following as was the usual lot of companions. Godfrey and Mary fell in behind her, Mary's hand comfortably settled on Godfrey's sleeve.

"So tell me of Miss Yardley," she asked, when they stood within the first shop, fingering any number of bolts of cloth and lace as they wandered from item to item.

Godfrey tilted his head back a little, a posture of recollection; it was clear he was gathering his thoughts. "Miss Yardley," he said slowly, then went on, "Miss Yardley is possibly the most available female I've ever known."

"No, she isn't. *I* am," Mary denied, though she felt a strong desire to stifle a giggle, only to be mildly ashamed of her own pleasure to find that Godfrey did not gush over the beautiful girl.

"Miss Yardley is to receive a dowry of some twenty thousand pounds."

Mary's eyes grew wide. It was an enormous sum.

"And a yearly income of two thousand pounds."

"Forever?"

"As long as her papa lives, yes."

"Goodness!"

"And unusual, a yearly stipend like that."

"But . . . but they *told* you these things?"

"Ah yes, quite directly in fact. But, it was my fault, for you see, I asked."

"You asked her father?" Mary said somewhat incredulously. Goodness! The Yardleys must be quite sure of Godfrey to be so upfront and direct.

"No, I asked the whole family. We were sitting around drinking tea, and it occurred to me to ask, and—even more incredibly—it occurred to them to answer. In front of dear Miss Yardley herself."

"Oh, Godfrey, no! You are jesting." Now Mary did giggle.

"I am not," he said, pretending to be slightly affronted. "And then they asked me how much I would bring to a union . . . if I just happened to fall into a union with . . . someone, you see."

"No!"

"Yes. So I told them. I thought one confidence deserved another. I believe I pleased them, if their happy faces were a reflection of their joy in the knowledge that I would not be a penniless suitor . . . for *someone,* of course."

Mary laughed aloud, undone by the sad efforts of Mrs. Pennett to refrain from giving away the fact that she was blatantly eavesdropping and therefore trying to prevent herself from chortling at the blatant gaucheries.

"And then I was asked if I cared to walk in the garden."

"Not by yourself, I think?" Mary asked, wide-eyed. She caught Mrs. Pennett's eye for a moment, and had to bite her lower lip to choke back another laugh.

"Oh no. Never a bit of it. All of us went out of doors, but then Lady Yardley remembered that she had not verified if the silver had been polished, and Lord Yardley suddenly recalled that he had meant to see about his hunter's foreleg, and — goodness! — I found myself alone in the gardens with their daughter, without so much as Miss Yardley's companion in attendance." His heavenly face was shaped into the contours of one who was utterly perplexed by events, a look so remarkably inapt for The Blade that even Mrs. Pennett gave up the fight and giggled along with her employer.

"Wh . . . what did you do?" Mary gasped, holding her side.

"Why, I suggested we return and look for the good lady."

"Oh, Godfrey! Oh, you didn't! How vexed she must have been."

"Not at all. She merely shook her head, smiling sweetly, and said, 'Miss Russell does not care for fresh air.' "

Other customers looked over to see two ladies leaning into each other, tears of mirth rolling down their faces, and a very handsome gentleman, his deep laughter rumbling through the establishment. Eventually, a variety of disapproving, shocked, scandalized, and even some mildly amused glances persuaded the trio to quit the shop, tumbling out into the street amidst another volley of laughter.

"See what you've done!" Mrs. Pennett tried to scold. "We'll never be able to show our faces in there again." But she grinned even as she said it.

"I *am* sorry I spoiled your search for a new gown."

"What's this? The Blade, apologizing?" a voice called. They turned to see it was Charles Bretwyn who approached them.

Godfrey took the hand that was extended to him, and they exchanged cordial greetings.

It was when Charles turned to Mary that Godfrey saw an unusual thing occur: Mary blushed delicately, and seemed unable to quite hold her head up. Godfrey turned to look at Charles again, and felt his own eyebrows lift as he saw the look of admiration there.

"How are you today?" he heard Charles asking.

"Quite well. And you, sir?" Mary asked quietly in return, looking up with a shy smile.

"Very well. I was out and about, in search of my special blend of tobacco, when I heard the delightful and unmistakable laughter of yourself."

Mary blushed again, and murmured something that no one understood.

Godfrey looked to Mrs. Pennett, and saw that the lady could have easily been the cat who ate the cream.

"What was it that made you so amused? No, I know it already. 'Twas Rothayne, of course." Charles moved forward, slipping past Godfrey to stand at Mary's side. In a twinkling her hand was on that gent's arm, and they were lost to conversation even as they moved away from the silent and abandoned duet left behind.

Godfrey looked again to Mrs. Pennett, but she had eyes only for her darling, and those eyes were one moment full of approval, and the next filled with something questioning. Godfrey had no idea what to make of the alternating expressions. When she looked back at him, she said, in a somewhat flustered manner that nonetheless spoke of her pleasure for her charge, "They look well together, don't they?"

Godfrey did not answer the question, his hands seeking out and burying themselves in his pockets. "Shall we?" he said, perhaps a little gruffly, indicating with his head that he meant to follow the couple talking together, their heads bent one toward the other.

They watched as Charles coaxed another smile from Mary. They watched as she reached out to touch the sleeve of his coat, directing his attention to something in a shop window. They watched as Charles took both her hands, gazed into her face, and said something earnest to her, something that made her lower her eyes again. Godfrey saw her take one quick, darting look in his direction, but then she had once again devoted herself to Charles' conversation.

At length, the course of shops had been reviewed, and the nattering pair turned at a corner, to await upon Godfrey and Mrs. Pennett. Charles made his good-byes then, and Mary saw him off with a smile.

Godfrey put himself out on the way home, regaling them with tales from his travels. He did not bring them once again to the point of exhaustive laughter, however, for a faint somber tone lay under his light tales. Finally, near the end of their ride, he turned to Mary, his eyes fixed on his grays, and casually said, "It seems Mr. Bretwyn is quite the interested *parti*."

Mary flushed again now, but it was not from any kind of pleasure. It had been awkward having Godfrey there to watch what honesty forced her to recognize was a new level of courtship from Mr. Bretwyn. "Yes," she said in a small voice.

"Did . . . did he say anything significant?"

167

"No, no. Just talk. He spoke of Letitia—"

"Letitia? Mrs. Hummold? You are calling her 'Letitia' these days?" He knew it came out boorishly, but she had surprised him. How chummy had Bretwyn and Mary become while he was gone? She should have explained to him how well things were advancing in that quarter.

"Yes. I'm sure I wrote to you that they bid me call them such."

"Them? Charles, too?" At Mary's wide-eyed nod, he cleared his throat and said a little too loudly, "Did you? Yes, I fancy you did."

"Anyway, Letitia has decided she wishes to be a patron of the arts. So, she is looking about for a suitable artist whom she can sponsor. Charles does not quite approve, I'm afraid. And he spoke of his dogs. You see, the lead female had to be put down. Distemper. He was quite upset, but what is one to do?"

"Yes, yes, but—" he cut himself off. He had been about to ask her why Charles had held her hands and spoken so earnestly to her, but that could have been the result of a loss of a favorite dog. And, besides, it had been their conversation, and he had no right to intrude upon it. "But," he finished somewhat lamely, "will you ride with me again tomorrow?"

"I cannot. I am promised to tea with Mrs. Rumshaw."

"The next day, then?"

"Oh, Godfrey, I am sorry, but I promised Charles and Letitia that I would be a fourth for cards. I hope you don't feel I'm trying to avoid you. I never would—"

"Of course not, love. But I've been home two

weeks and I've only had the pleasure of your company four times."

"Greedy," Mrs. Pennett threw in.

Godfrey gave the companion a steady look, but she was not the slightest bit cowed. If anything she gave him back a look that made him look away, wondering for a second why the thought crossed his mind that she might as well have added the words "and stupid". It was particularly startling because one did not expect such a look from a mere companion, and because it was much like the other strange looks she had been casting his way of late. To shake off the impression that Mrs. Pennett was trying to get something through to a particularly thick child, he turned back to Mary, and said, "Don't promise away *all* your time, or I'll begin to believe I'm back in Kent, with no dear Mary in sight."

Mary laughed then, and the mood in the carriage lightened, as was inevitable whenever they laughed together. It had been uncomfortable, this unusual constraint between them. Almost as uncomfortable as having to conduct her growing relationship with Charles under Godfrey's keen eyes. It was difficult, for with Charles she acted one way, and with Godfrey another, more direct way. But that way, after all, was what he had always insisted upon, and he ought not to take it amiss if she acted more properly with others. Indeed, she thought somewhat militantly, what business of his was it if she had chosen even to be an outright hypocrite? She need spare no blushes for the inanities that society forced her to utter, the "ladylike" conduct that was expected, not if those things meant Charles was to be drawn to her. This other relationship, with Godfrey, now *there* was the odd one! No, she must not follow her instincts, the

169

ones that cried out to be far and away from those bright blue, searching eyes whenever she happened to be in Charles Bretwyn's company. Of course Godfrey would have to be a witness to such, and if she felt any awkwardness, well, she must simply make herself *not* do so.

She avoided Mrs. Pennett's gaze, as did Godfrey, for the remainder of the ride.

Chapter Fifteen

Mary stepped away from her partner, her cheeks slightly flushed from their exertions, and the lieutenant's conversation. He might be a trifle dull when it came to discussing a number of subjects, but one had merely to breathe a word of "the army" or "politics", and suddenly he was erudite and witty, a repository of any number of sparkling tales from his military experiences.

"Sir, you make me believe I have been to India myself," Mary complimented him.

"I should think you would enjoy India. Not every woman can adapt, but I know you would see beyond the beggars and the uncleanliness, and see much of the beauty that I have seen there."

His eyes glowed as he spoke, as much for her as for India, she fancied. The compliment, and the hint of more than mere approval were not lost on her. She was therefore in the best of moods when a late entrance was made. It was hard to miss the occurrence, for a ripple spread through the crowd, bringing more than just Mary's eyes in the direction of their hostess, who stood greeting the latecomer.

It was none other than Miss Yardley, which in and of itself was unexpected, but then, too, there was

Godfrey as escort, with Miss Yardley's hand plainly set upon his sleeve.

Mary was not aware that her smile had faded; she did not realize that the blood drained from her face, and that she had caught her lower lip between her teeth. She knew, however, that the dark head so near the fiery glory of Godfrey's own made for a remarkably striking picture, and she heard the murmurs of assent to that fact all around her.

"I'm here for my dance," Lord Faver said near her, causing her to jump. She'd had no idea he was there.

"Yes," she said a little unsteadily, but when he took her in his arms, she was glad that he had come for her. It gave her time to recover from her surprise, and to paste a smile back on her face. Somehow she found herself speaking of the very thing that had nonplussed her. "Do you know the lady who has just arrived?"

Lord Faver glanced in the direction of the dark-haired beauty, and said simply, "No."

"Well, I do. She is Miss Yardley."

"Annalee Yardley? Of the Kent Yardleys?" Lord Faver asked, his young face reflecting only a mild curiosity.

"Yes, she must be. I did not know her Christian name. We met in the country. Do you wish for an introduction?" Mary asked, almost biting her tongue as soon as the words came out. What was she thinking of—offering to make introductions? Well, why shouldn't she? They *were* acquaintances. It was just that she had not expected to see the lady . . . or Godfrey . . . tonight. *What a ninny!* she chided herself, vowing she would recover her poise right now. Right this minute. Immediately.

"I'm sorry, what did you say?" she suddenly recalled herself and realized that Lord Faver had answered her, and she had not heard him.

"I said 'No, thank you'. I want nothing to do with a high flyer such as her."

"Why, Thomas, you surprise me! A high flyer, indeed. What do you think *you* are, if not a high flyer?"

"I'm not, Lady Wagnall, not a bit of it. I know I'm far too bookish, and serious-minded. The ladies tell me so all the time. They laugh at me, and tell me it's a good thing I can dance, as I cannot speak."

"Thomas . . .!"

"No, it's true. Some fellows have the gift of gab, but I do not. Not in a crowd like this, anyway. Oh, with you it's different, because you're not . . ."

"A high flyer?" she supplied for him, one eyebrow arched, but her smile softened the effect.

"Well, no. Dash it all, you know what I mean! Such as right now. Most ladies would give me a rap with their fans and never speak to me again, but I know *you* won't take umbrage, and make me squirm and feel like a buffoon. You might laugh, but it would be kind laughter, you understand?" he finished, obviously aggravated.

"Well, I thank you for the compliments, Thomas. And as a favor, I will take you away to the punch bowl, where we both may linger and watch the goings-on."

He approved heartily, if his relieved expression was anything by which to judge, and they found themselves quite unmolested for half an hour behind the punch bowl. In time, when she spied a singularly inoffensive and passive girl, Miss Lupton, she made the efforts required to set the two together for a dance. Seeing them safely among the other dancers, Mary sighed and made as if to move among the matrons and take a seat for a bit of a spell, but it was

173

not to be. For when she turned in that direction, she all but collided with Godfrey.

"I have been looking for you for hours," he said.

"Hardly that. You only arrived a half an hour ago, or so."

"So you noticed? I did not think you had. Did you save me any dances, you scamp? Or has Charles signed up for all of them?" he asked, lifting her card from where it dangled off her wrist. "Oho, what's this? Why is this card so blank?"

"I have been tending my friend, Lord Faver, poor pup. He would be the happiest of lads if he could only bring himself to find some nice, steady girl to marry."

"Yes, I had heard there were fellows such as he, ones that actually *desire* the end of bachelorhood."

"You are the matchmaking expert here. Perhaps you should see that he meets the right girl," Mary said, warming up to their usual bantering style.

"One match at a time, dear girl. Speaking of which, is Charles not here tonight?"

"No, he is very involved right now in his investments. He deplores the fact that it means his absence, but duty calls, so he 'must away'."

"Then I will take several of his dances."

"Just two. Any more than that, and Miss Yardley would have to look elsewhere for a husband."

"Mary, Mary," Godfrey shook his head mournfully. "You are forever squelching my attempts to ruin you."

"Duty calls," she repeated, smiling. "But what of Miss Yardley? Have you so soon abandoned her?"

"Never that," Godfrey said, looking over his shoulder to where a knot of gentlemen stood. "I am afraid that Miss Yardley is swamped with offers of dance partners right now. 'Tis why I chose to arrive with her, that I might have first choice at her card, before it was filled up."

"When did she arrive in London?" Mary asked, biting back the additional questions of "how" and "why."

"This morning. She sent me a note, as I am one of her few acquaintances in London. Mary, did you know she is only sixteen?"

"Truly?" Mary asked, her face registering her surprise. "Hers is not the round-cheeked beauty of great youth. I admit I would have guessed at least several years more."

"It does rather explain why she seems . . . shy at times. I do not think her parents intended for her to have a season this year."

Until you came into their orbit, Mary said to herself.

"And why she seems . . . sometimes unclear as to what she means to be saying."

So you noticed her blatant/innocent combination, did you? Mary thought. And what was that dancing light in his eyes: was that amusement, or was that understanding? Attraction, perhaps? Mary looked back toward the group, catching an occasional glimpse of the fluttering, smiling Miss Yardley. Perhaps. Perhaps Hortense was right, and it would take this particular kind of female to bring Godfrey to the altar. He could not help but notice how much stir she had caused already, just by making an appearance. Such a pretty creature could easily become an incomparable, with a little luck and a little skill. If the Duke wished it, he could lend his talents in that direction . . . and what man would not want a woman he was thinking of taking to wife to be the greatest success?

"My dance, dearest. The music is beginning,"

Godfrey said to her, taking up her hand in his. As usual, his touch sent a shiver up and down her arm, but she went into his arms without allowing herself to think on it.

After the dance, he excused himself. "To check on my protegée," he explained.

Mary noted that Charles made a belated entry, but was glad when it was only she and Mrs. Pennett who drove home together. She could not have borne any company, not even Godfrey's. Thankfully Gladys seemed lost to her own thoughts.

Mary could not know that Mrs. Pennett had spent well over an hour in Mr. Bretwyn's company. She had struck up a conversation with him, drawing him into an alcove that others might not steal him away for a dance. She had seen too much in her charge's eyes, seen things that worried her. If she had ever seen those same things in Lord Rothayne's eyes, she might not have worried so, but whenever his eyes had met hers over Mary's innocent head, he had given her a big, blank look that spoke volumes. His lack of comprehension had spurred her on, reminded her that Mary was seeking a husband, not a mere friend, and that she, Gladys Pennett, had sworn to find such for the girl, and the sooner the better. The season was winding down; time was running short. There was no time for mere games; it was time to have a declaration, from one gentlemen if not the other. And the one was so much more likely than the other, so far as husband-making material went.

So she had cornered Mr. Bretwyn, running a list of Mary's attributes up one of his sides and down the other. He, being a gentleman, had kindly agreed with her, and had even been so bold, and frankly encouraged, as to utter a few words of praise for the lady himself, until Mrs. Pennett actually asked him what were his intentions.

"Well . . . er . . . that is to say . . . my intentions, you ask?" Charles had sputtered.

"Yes. Quite."

"I . . . uh . . . well, to tell you the truth, Mrs. Pennett, I have not been all that convinced that Lady Wagnall has set her heart in my direction. In point of fact, I have wondered if she and Lord Ro—"

"But, Mr. Bretwyn, this is why I asked to speak with you! I was worried that Mary's natural shyness would manifest itself as a sign of indifference. I must tell you, she speaks of you all the time when we are alone together. She tells me how kind you are, how cultured, how well-read," she went on, adding any number of compliments, some of which Mary had actually uttered.

Mr. Bretwyn colored in an attractive, flattered fashion, and murmured, "Does she, by Jove?"

Mrs. Pennett assured him it was true.

He shrugged, and half-laughed, embarrassed to be discussing such a matter with a companion, but doing so anyway, a tell-tale sign to Mrs. Pennett's sharp eyes. "But how I am to know these things for myself?" he finally asked, the tips of his ears still scarlet at the abundant praise she heaped upon his head.

"Well, you've only to ask if she'll marry you. Either answer will tell you the truth, won't it?" Mrs. Pennett said, and her eyes actually glowed when Mr. Bretwyn somewhat hesitantly nodded.

After that she had let him go, unable to do more to promote her darling Mary. She had planted the seed—no, she had planted a seedling!—and now she could only stand back and watch to see whether it would bloom and grow, or not.

* * *

"Mary," Charles said. She looked over at him, at the seriousness of his tone. Over their heads, another elegant display from a fireworks rocket exploded, momentarily lighting their features before they settled back into only indistinct shades of gray. He put a hand on her sleeve, pulling her back a few steps, so they were near to neither Mrs. Hummold nor Mrs. Pennett. "Will you marry me, then, Mary?" he asked in a low voice, near her ear, that she might hear him over the sound of the exploding fireworks.

She had been prepared for the question for some time now, and had thought she had the answer ready on her lips. Yet now she found that she waited for another aerial display to pass into memory, waited for her heart to cease squeezing the breath from her lungs, before she nodded her head silently in the dark and managed to answer, "Yes."

His hand came over hers, squeezing gently. For a moment, she thought she might shake him off, might cry out "No!", but the moment passed. Even though her eyes were softly kissed with the dew of tears, she knew a kind of gratitude to him, that he had made this offer to keep time with her, and give her that which she had longed for for so long. If the moment was bittersweet, well, what more had she expected?

"We'll tell the others on the way home."

"Yes, all right," she whispered, not aware that she flinched every time another firework exploded over her head.

Chapter Sixteen

She walked her horse beside Godfrey's, a not completely comfortable silence between them. It was the first truly sunny day they had had all season long. At last the rain clouds had rolled away. There was no possibility that either of them would not have been out in the day's warm caress, and she had been both elated and then sickened in her heart when he came to her door and asked her to ride with him. For, of course, she would have to tell him of the betrothal, and she dreaded that. Not that he would be upset—far from it, of course—but to speak of her engagement aloud, to him, would then be to make it real. That the sun shone down on their heads so gaily seemed a cruel joke of nature upon her mangled feelings.

She had come out with him at once, disdaining even to ask Mrs. Pennett to ride with them. That lady had looked at her as though she had grown a second head when she revealed that she had accepted Mr. Bretwyn's offer.

"And that's why you cried all night long?" Mrs. Pennett had asked piercingly.

Mary had winced, not knowing her storm of tears

179

had been overheard. "It is emotional, becoming betrothed," she had answered.

Gladys's face had contorted in several different ways, but finally she had managed to say, "I'm sure he's a fine man, Mr. Bretwyn."

So Mary had not invited her companion along today. She was, after all, a betrothed woman now, so she would allow herself this one little bit of leniency — a last time alone with Godfrey, completely alone.

Godfrey commented occasionally on what manner of bird was singing with gay abandon in a nearby tree, or stooped to see if a flower held any scent, or talked to his horse, assuring the beast that he would have another chance to run soon. They had chosen to ride the streets of London, and when they were outside of Mayfair, they elected to give the beasts their heads. It was not done, of course, and that only made it all the more exhilarating. Now they walked, letting the animals regain their wind, or perhaps it was themselves they wished to pamper a little. Mary grew in appreciation for the peacefulness of the day — it proved to be a balm to ruffled emotions and an unsteady mind, for though she had made her decision, it had nagged at her all this past night and into this day.

She watched Godfrey, drinking in the sight of him as she knew she would seldom, if ever, have the chance to do once she was married. She allowed shivers to run up and down her spine, not stifled nor dwelled upon, but merely a fact of life and time such as it was right now, right this minute. Today it was at first his hands she noted; they were strong, capable, their movements reflecting the wealth of knowledge and experience behind that well-formed forehead.

His natural refinement was even seen in so little a thing as the way he held the reins — was there ever a more graceful man born? Then there was the way his long legs stretched out as he walked, the angle of his head as he listened to the sounds around him, how he lifted an arm to point out some place to her — everything filled her eyes, her ears, her thoughts, until she had to close her eyes and tell herself, yet again, to recall that invisible window between them, a window now well and truly frosted by the agreement she had made with Charles.

They came to a stretch of road that was not flanked by houses, and it was plain he wished to stop and linger a while. She slid at once from her horse, bruising the bottom of her foot on a stone, so eager had she been to keep him from touching her in an assist from her mount.

"I wonder what district this is?" he said, turning around in the middle of the road, trying to find a hint.

"I don't know," she said as she also gazed about. It was a lovely shaded spot, with trees that lowered their leaves in places so that they almost touched the road.

"It's rather amazing, not so far outside of the center of town, to find such a slow road."

"Look at those ruts, though. I don't wonder there is plenty of traffic in the mornings."

"Ah, you're correct." He led his horse to the side of the road, draping the reins over a low branch. She followed his lead, and then together they found a large rock whose uneven surface offered them each a place to sit. There was a thin stream that rolled along the ground before them, where only the many days of rain could have made a stream, and Godfrey absently scooped up pebbles and tossed them, to disappear beneath the surface of the swift little current.

"You are quiet this morning," he said, pausing at his task to look at her fully. The sunlight burnished his hair to a bright copper, that striking halo of near-gold gilding the darker color, and his eyes were the exact same shade as the morning sky above him.

"I have something to tell you."

"I thought as much. You are not going to tell me you are bored with my simple, wicked ways, are you? I shall try harder to be more deviant, if you should so desire."

She smiled then, and shook her head softly. It took her a moment to find the words, but at length she said quietly, "Charles has asked me to marry him."

For a moment he did nothing, not even to take a breath, but then he began throwing pebbles again. "Did you give him an answer?" he asked, staring at the place where the stones sank from view.

"I said yes."

He nodded a few times, brief, concise little nods. "I must be the first to wish you happy," he said, suddenly coming to his feet. He leaned forward then, rather stiffly, like a boy made to greet an unpopular aunt, and pressed a kiss upon her right cheek. "Charles is a lucky man," he said as he stood. "May you have every happiness together, my dear." He stepped back, his hands falling motionless to his sides.

She gave him a wavery smile which faded quickly. Before her throat tightened completely, she managed to get out, "Thank you."

He took a few steps around the clearing, almost as if he were pacing. Suddenly he said, "Well, my, this rather changes things, doesn't it? Charles would not care to have me forever whisking you off to one escapade or another, I feel sure. But not to worry! I shall take myself a wife, and the four of us may arrange to have our paths cross frequently."

"I should . . ." she blinked furiously, refusing to cry, refusing to admit to herself she had wished for something much different than words of congratulations from him. Silly, of course, to have even pretended, even imagined that he would declare that his own affection for her ran too deep to allow her to marry another. Oh, it was an old, silly dream, one she had rightfully dismissed when first they met, and yet, bidden or not, a dream that has been extinguished must result in some pain, as if the ashes of her dreams were what caused her eyes to smart so sharply. "I should like that," she managed to say.

"Well, it's time we headed back, isn't it?" he said briskly. He crossed to her horse, and stood at the ready. "Come, I'll help you mount."

He cupped his hands, ready for the small foot she slid there after shakily rising to her feet. The feel of his hands on her, even through the kid slipper, was an unexpected agony, and she had to close her eyes and not think, and trust he would not throw her over the saddle. Once settled, albeit after a wild thump, she dared to open her eyes, only to find him staring up at her. "Mary? Are you hurt?"

"Jitters," she said through gritted teeth. "Wedding jitters, 'tis all."

"I can believe it. When I think of taking my own vows, I nearly faint with— Mary!" he cried out as she suddenly kicked her horse and flipped the reins, causing the animal to surge past him.

"It's a race. Meet you at the park!" she called over

her shoulder. Perhaps, by the time he caught up with her, the fast pace would explain her flushed face and teary eyes.

But when he had nearly ridden abreast of her, suddenly the sight of his precious face, of the habitual amusement in his eyes, of even just the way he lifted a hand to hail her, was more than she could bear. "I must be off! See you later, Godfrey!" she called, again spurring her horse forward, away from those earthly eyes of a fallen angel, lightest blue and clever, too clever to deceive for long when tears choked her throat.

When she arrived home, she found her companion waiting for her in her room. "You've been riding with the duke?" Mrs. Pennett asked, and her slightly worried, questioning look was at once replaced by uncertainty when she saw her charge's lower lip quiver. Mary tried to bluff for a moment, but then the tears slid from her eyes, and she found herself in Mrs. Pennett's caring arms, well aware by the distressed look on the woman's face that her companion had guessed her secret. Mrs. Pennett made some distressed noises over her bowed and weeping head, and went on to murmur, "Hush now, love. Life is funny. Mr. Bretwyn and you will suit just fine, you'll see. Hush now." But there were tears in her eyes as well, tears for Mary's heartache, and tears of regret that she had been so imprudent as to meddle.

"Lord Yardley, Lady Yardley. How does the day find you?" Godfrey greeted the pair as he was ushered into their London home.

"Oh, quite well, your grace. And all the better for your unexpected visit today," Lady Yardley said with enthusiasm.

184

Godfrey refused to be annoyed by her fawning; one corner of his mouth rose in a ghost of a smile. "I am welcome then?" he asked, knowing that if they noted the slight hint of sarcasm in his tone, they would choose to ignore it.

"Of course, of course. Always. Let me just nip upstairs, to let Annalee know you are here. We won't be but a minute."

It was, in fact, thirty-five minutes before the lady reappeared, her freshly dressed and coifed daughter in tow. Godfrey blinked, keeping his face free of his amazement to see that the girl was wearing dampened draperies at ten in the morning. Of course it was all the style, but one seldom encountered the look in broad daylight. If he had had any doubts before, now it was quite clear to him—and indeed anyone in the world who should happen to enter the room—that Miss Annalee Yardley was endowed with sweetly rounded breasts, set high, the posture and position of her darkened nipples only half-obscured. Gone was the bit of lace that might have hid her cleavage. Gone was the shawl that might have hinted at but never actually revealed, as now, the bounty beneath the shimmering gauze of her gown. Godfrey found himself pressing his lips together, and a glance at Lord Yardley showed him that the fellow took it as a sign of appreciation, rather than the truer act of struggling to suppress a loud guffaw. He began to have a sense of how young female lovelies must feel when they were blatantly wooed and pursued by those of his own gender. It was not a comfortable thing, this forwardness of manner, not for the recipient.

That thought sobered him, for he knew full well that it was possible that Miss Annalee wanted him for little more than his title and his comely countenance. He recalled that before this day, words of love he had uttered had proved to be no more than the mere sighs of physical attraction, which, he knew full well, was never love. Was this fetching creature old enough to even desire the comfort and security of a loving relationship? Was she, in fact, old enough to *love?*

"I wondered if I might have a stroll about the garden with you again, Miss Yardley?" he asked blatantly.

"Certainly, certainly," interjected her father as the lady in question took on a glowing look of eagerness. "You wouldn't care for a brandy first, would you?" Lord Yardley added, obviously hoping to take Godfrey aside long enough to grant his blessings.

"It's a bit too early for me, sir," Godfrey replied drolly, verbally sidestepping the invitation.

The lord and his lady exchanged looks. "I'll see if I can locate Miss Russell," Lady Yardley said, referring to the often absent chaperone. Lady Yardley moved from the room at once. *No doubt to an upstairs window,* Godfrey thought to himself, placed there to watch them walk the lengths of the garden. From such a vantage point, the companion and the mama could determine together whether or not the precious daughter of the house was actually in need of the saving company of her companion.

Annalee accepted his arm, and he thought for a moment that perhaps he ought to insist on a shawl for her, but then he mentally shrugged, and told himself she was young and healthy enough to withstand the effects of a cool breeze on a wetted gown. And if the garden light provided yet further glimpses of the lady's form, well that had not been of his arranging, now had it?

Sunlight was kind to the youthful skin and dark hair of the lady. Her cheeks began to glow a healthy pink at the touch of the breeze, and her dark hair glinted almost silver where the rays of light touched her head. Soft curls fell about her face, while the bulk of her hair was pulled back and up, giving her a slightly older look, and yet still it was easy to see her great youth. Her hand on his sleeve was almost weightless, a reflection of her delicate construction, and her dark eyes were bright with a kind of excitement he was not too cynical to take as a compliment.

The time had come upon him — not quite set in stone, but still feeling heavy as one hung about his neck — when he must decide about the chit. She was ravishing, of that there could be no doubt, and she also obviously admired some, if not all, aspects of his own person and company, but could the girl *speak?* Or, rather, could she entertain, enlighten, amuse, challenge, set verbal sparks stinging about his ears, and cause him to listen to more than every other word she said? It was not fair to expect too much, for such youth must of necessity know less of the world than an old rake such as himself, but one could hope for signs of future talents, couldn't one?

"Annalee, tell me about yourself." It was a flat sort of thing to say, not his usual flattering way with women, but along with the decision to decide had come the lack of desire to play at games.

"Oh, there is not much to tell," she answered. She had a pleasant voice, but her answer grated on his nerves slightly. It was exactly the answer any other girl would have given. It flashed through his mind that Mary would have gaily launched into a storm of words, telling and showing him exactly what she was

187

made of, but Mary was the exception to the rule, and therefore could not be used as the measure by which others were compared.

"No, in truth, Annalee, I wish to know something of you. Take, for instance . . ." he thought a moment, and settled on, "do you have any pets?"

"Papa has his hunting dogs, of course. He lets me feed them bits of beef sometimes. They adore Papa."

"Do you play with them?"

"Play?" she laughed, a slight look of genuine surprise coming to her features. "I'm no longer a school miss, your grace," she said. "Of course I do not *play* with the dogs!" She shook her head at the silliness of the question, but sensing something of his mood, she hastened to add, "Do you care for dogs, your grace?"

"Care for? I haven't any of my own, but, yes, I guess you could say I have a care for dogs in general. I, too, grew up with hunting dogs. My father was very indulgent of them, and they had the run of the house. I used to ride upon the backs of the larger ones, until I grew too big for that, and had to settle for merely running with the pack." He smiled at the memory.

"You . . . you ran with the dogs? Through the house?" she said hesitantly, a smile flickering in and out of existence around her mouth.

"Indeed I did. Would you care to hear me howl? I am quite good at it. I can get a pack of almost any breed going."

She blinked slowly, then nodded, equally slowly. "Yes, of course, if you like, your grace."

"Call me Godfrey, please," he said, even as he pushed aside the idea of giving his demonstration, not unaware of the lady's resistance to the very thought of a duke howling in her backyard. You could read the mixture of resignation and bewilderment on her face. Instead he went on, "Tell me, have you ever traveled?"

"Oh yes!" she cried with enthusiasm, obviously relieved with the change of topic. "My parents have taken me to Brussels, France, Prussia, and Italy. I speak a little of the three languages, but I am only truly proficient in French. I did so enjoy seeing all the capitols. Rome was fascinating, even if Papa was very uncomfortable in the midst of 'all that Papacy,' as he called it. Brussels was beautiful, but very cold when we were there. And Paris! Paris was simply heavenly! How I admired all the shops. Everything is so *au courant*. I felt a perfect dowd, though my gowns were new just for the "grand tour", as Papa called it. And such hats! To put on a French *chapeau* is to never want to wear another plain English poke bonnet in your life!"

"Did you attend any of the night life? I myself was always partial to simply strolling the *Champs Elysees* after dark, for that is when the city truly shows its face."

"Oh no, I would never venture out after dark, not in a strange city."

"But if I were to escort you? Keep you safe from any indecent types?" he said, teasing lightly, pleased to see she was not completely void of the ability to converse.

He had expected her to smile and nod, so he was startled when she cried, "Oh no, I could not. Papa says it would be unsafe. And not only that, it would also cause others to question my judgement, if not my virtue."

"But if you and I —?" he cut himself short, not

wanting to say exactly "if we should be married."

"Your grace?"

"If we were alone. Without your papa around. At all."

"Without Papa? Why would I go to Paris without Papa?"

He gave a half-laugh, not sure what to make of her ingenuity—was he glad she did not leap, as others might, to matrimonial thoughts, or was he merely amazed at her thickheadedness? Could it be a ruse, a clever act of innocence? If so, that in itself was not all bad, for it showed she had sharp wits.

"Ah, well, as to that . . ." he said, allowing the words to trail away. He shook his head, and turned the conversation even as he turned them down a side path in the garden. "What do you care to do of a day, Annalee?"

As she began to describe a typical day, he found himself frowning mildly, listening with only half an ear, as he tried to understand his tolerance of the girl. Normally he had no time for fools, but then again, he was far from convinced that she *was* a fool. No, no, he could not mistake youthful incomprehension for foolishness. She was, as Mary had once said, merely *gauche,* in the same way that a new colt was *gauche,* and such simple, honest *gaucherie* was easily cured by time. She had the refinement of her raising, and if that could be coupled with a little polish and knowledge, she would be an admirable hostess and companion, he did not doubt.

". . . And I often spend at least an hour at the pianoforte, practicing my playing, and another hour with my voice instructor. I cannot like him, for he is harsh in his manners, but he has helped me to improve my voice."

190

"Ah, you sing. Would you sing some little thing for me now?" Godfrey asked, coming back from his wandering thoughts to latch unto this latest revelation.

"Oh, I could not, your grace," Annalee said shyly, flushing a light, pretty pink.

"Certainly you could. Who is there to hear? Your neighbors? I doubt it, and even if so, then they shall just have to endure us at our leisure."

"No, honestly, your grace . . ."

"I tell you what. I shall embarrass myself first, so that you may easily best my efforts. How does that sound?"

She did not shake nor nod her head, so he began to sing anyway. He sang "Lads, to Your Steeds, Away, Away", his voice fine but not excellent, and when he finished he was able to smile at her and say, "Now it is your turn."

She shook her head.

"Come now, you would not want me to be alone in my embarrassment, would you?"

Other ladies might have answered "Yes", to make him laugh, or "No", to make an end of the matter, but Annalee seemed uncertain, unable to answer either way, and so he pressed again.

"Come now."

"I should . . . I mean . . ." she stammered.

"A little ditty. Nothing much."

"It is so disconcerting. To sing in the garden!" she cried.

"Try it. The novelty is refreshing."

Finally she agreed. She sang "Fair Bonnie Maid, of Upton Glade". Her voice, well trained, was pretty and even, though not truly perfect, and lacking in emotion. Still, he was sincere when he complimented

191

her efforts, even though he could not help but recall the clarity and emotional appeal of Mary Wagnall's gifted voice.

They walked a while longer, and he asked her all kinds of questions about her youth (a thought which made him smile secretly, for he was not entirely convinced that it could be said her youth was behind her), and came to learn the lady knew much about the management of a household. She had been well-schooled by her mama, who appeared to be only slightly less — he thought to himself with another smile — an authority on all matters than the girl's papa. He knew, even as he smiled, that it was quite the thing for her to think so well of her parents, and indeed what other experience of life had she been given by which to judge? He found that she had a sincere love of painting, and when he escorted her into the house, she took him on a tour of her works, well represented in the rooms of the household.

After a fair time had passed, he bid the lady and her parents farewell, put on his curly crowned beaver, and climbed into his carriage, firmly sure of his decision in the matter of marriage to Miss Annalee Yardley.

Chapter Seventeen

When next Mary and Godfrey met it was at her betrothal party.

She had not seen him, not even across the park, in three weeks. Now, gone were her tears, replaced by a calm and composed demeanor. His sister, Hortense, had arrived before him. Her greeting had been all that it should be, but Mary fancied she had detected just a touch of censure from the other lady. Mary had gone on to accept the best wishes of thirty or forty other souls before he walked through her door, eclipsing everyone else in the room — yes, even Charles. But that was not to be wondered at, for she did not love Charles, and she did love Godfrey.

That fact was inescapable to her since she had lain all night weeping copiously into her pillow, trying to smother and hide the sounds of torment, especially from the ears of her companion, only one room away. She thought perhaps she had always known it, but there had been a time when she thought she could simply will it away. What a lie! What a fool's dream!

Now it was all that she could do to appear as composed as if he were the fishmonger delivering his wares, and not her heart's desire. She was able to look him in the face, if not exactly in the eye, to form a smile, to say softly that he was looking well, all the while immensely aware of Charles at her elbow. She wanted to ask Godfrey where he had been, but that would not have been fair. He had called twice at her home, both times when she was out and about on errands for this very party. She could have sent him a note or two, telling him when to find her at home, but she had not, so it was decidedly unfair to even think to accuse him of avoiding her.

But all her carefully arranged thoughts fell to nothing when he took her hands between his own, and leaned forward to place a light kiss on her cheek. She had read in books of women who, tortured by the pangs of love, had behaved as nothing more intelligent than geese, and finally she knew that it could be so. Her thoughts were shattered, her composure in shreds, her ability to smile, even idiotically, erased.

"Mary, I wish you well," he said, and then he hesitated. He gave a kind of tiny shrug of his shoulders, his hands tugging slightly at hers. He then walked away, leaving her devastated, but not so completely that she had missed a certain light in his eyes, a light she did not know, had never seen before. It was not anger, nor irritation, nor judgement. She had seen those things on his face before. This was . . . something softer than those others, yet just as intense.

When she turned to Charles, the light in his eyes was different, too, not his usual open, friendly, pleasant gaze. He looked either annoyed or confused, or perhaps both or neither. In her confused state she could not say. When she forced a smile up at him, the look faded and he smiled in return. As he turned to greet another guest, she closed her own eyes for a moment, willing away cognizance, praying for a blissful state of numbness. It came to her, not completely, but in a fashion that allowed her to smile and nod, rather as though she was watching another person performing the duties for her.

Dinner was served once everyone had arrived. Mary felt the food slide down her throat, knew enough to nod and attempt a smile or two when the many toasts were raised to she and Charles, and felt the warm touch of the wine as it floated into her veins, but still she seemed to be standing a little beside herself, half-marveling at her own talent for maintaining an outwardly calm demeanor. Though it was true she could not think what to say, and so said nothing at all, everyone must have taken her silence as either a variety of shy gentility or perhaps bride-to-be jitters. None chastised her for her silence, nor did they even try to coax forward more than a collection of singular words from her. Charles, seated next to her at the broad end of the long formal table, was quite verbose enough for both of them, and even she had to smile slightly once or twice at the quips and tales he shared with such easy abandon with the table.

Godfrey, seated many seats from Mary's side, looked up once or twice to give Mary a nod or a smile, but mostly he gave his attention to those seated around him. She saw, however, that near the end of the meal he excused himself from the table, and that he did not return.

Servants came to light the many tapers of the overhead chandeliers against the approaching gloom of nightfall, and the many sconces scattered around the room, just prior to the arrival of a large and elaborately frosted cake. The many tiers were arranged to look like an impossible set of grand stairs, bedecked with all manner of flora, fauna, and winged cherubim leading up to the church at the top, which was out of all proportion to the stairs that led up to it. The church's doors were open, and a tiny marzipan bride and groom were just stepping out its doors, hand in hand. The party of well-wishers murmured at the sight of it, and then broke into applause, saluting the chef's master work as well as the couple for whom it was intended to celebrate. Charles' hand slipped over Mary's, but she found she could not turn her head and look to him, could not smile, and so she settled on merely leaving her hand where it lay under his. Again she felt the need to close her eyes and hide away from everything and everyone in the room.

Charles and she were the first served, and when she had raised a bite of the cake to her lips, the gentleman on her right asked her if it was tasty. She nodded, and though her fork pretended to be busy on her plate, not another morsel could she bring to pass her lips.

It was with an enormous sense of relief that she found the men now wished to take their port, pulling Charles along with them to drink to his health and that of his lady. The relief was not long standing, though, for the ladies were just as inclined to surround the bride-to-be, and she found herself at last having to crawl from her virtual silence to answer a hundred questions on where they would live, and what she would wear, and how did they meet? It kept her mind busy; at least she could say that for the assault.

* * *

Godfrey knew the house well enough to easily find the most deserted room. It was at the back of the house, far removed from the gaiety in the front rooms. Longing as he did for solitude, he had made his way without a candle. The room was dark as the night outside, unlighted by either a lamp or a fire on the grate. There was no need to close the door after himself. No one could see him here. The darkness was as soothing as the remoteness of the room itself. The night was still, not exactly warm, but still he found himself longing for the night breezes. He crossed to the double french doors located to the right of the entrance, drew back the curtains, and threw open the doors. He leaned against the door-frame, letting the fresh air touch the skin of his face and hands, pulling it into his lungs as though he had been deprived for some while of its sweet flow. He let the night sounds — of both the house and the garden beyond — override his own jumbled thoughts. He allowed the sounds to caress his ears, hearing them without trying to comprehend them. It was a kind of music, soothing, steadying. The three-quarters moon was still low in the sky, but its light was not obscured by even the tiniest of clouds, so that once his eyes adjusted, there was much that could be seen. Inside, a chair, a desk, a pile of unorganized books, while out of doors he saw gray shadow blossoms nodding in the night breeze, saw the pattern of the trellis, and the glistening in the distance that indicated a body of water. It was a scene of serenity, and yet, he knew he was not really a part of such a vastly desired thing as serenity.

And so, despite his attempt to find a measure of peace, he was not startled when a voice invaded the darkness.

"There's the good lad!" Charles said from the doorway, holding a lighted candlestick aloft. He squinted through the gloom, the small light only serving to make the darkness more apparent.

"You were looking for me?" Godfrey made no move to come away from the doorframe. So here was one of the very players that was disturbing his mind, making him restless in a way he had not been in many a year.

Charles strode into the room, the light revealing a face not over-filled with joviality, so that Godfrey knew, if he had not before from the tone, that Charles had come with a specific purpose in mind. Charles went on, saying calmly, "I think we should talk. Say what we would, eh?"

"Yes," Godfrey said at once, allowing his relief at the lack of need for pretense to come into his answer.

"It's about Mary, of course," Charles said.

"Yes," Godfrey agreed again. "You must know that she is very special to me."

"I know it. I'll tell you true, your grace, there was more than once when I thought perhaps I should step aside, let you have the girl. But then, at other times I got the distinct feeling that even if I did you'd not make a move in that direction."

Godfrey looked back to the garden, as though to assess the quality of the roses whose color he could only guess at, but then he turned those glowing orbs once more to the room. He said simply, "I doubt I would have, at that."

Charles turned his head a little, in the way a dog does when it hears a far and faint sound. "I hope . . . you realize of course that a man must declare himself at some point or other? One cannot string a woman along forever. That is to say . . ." his voice trailed away, perhaps reluctant to define if it was himself or the duke of which he spoke.

"Charles," Godfrey said on a sigh, for the man had been one of his few friends for some years now, and he hated the thought of the unwanted but nonetheless tangible restraints that had sprung between them this night. "I know it is wrong-headed of me to speak, but I want you to understand how easily Mary could be hurt. I want to be sure in my own mind that you know the manner of temperament which is hers. She's been . . . overlooked for too long. She would not stand up well under those conditions which are normal in most households. The mistresses. The lengthy leaves. Liquor, gambling, all of it. She could not abide to be used and forgotten. If you want just a brood mare, then I beg you, do not take *this* woman to wife . . ." His words trailed away, for there was so much more he wanted to say, so many cautions and restrictions and guidelines, all of which he had absolutely no right to utter.

"I'm not an oaf," Charles said, a crackle of anger in his voice.

"No. No, of course you're not."

"I know how to treat a woman."

"She won't be just 'a woman'. She'll be your wife. She'll expect . . . so much. She would deny it, if she heard it said, for she believes herself capable of a marriage of convenience, but in truth she would look to you, expecting fidelity. Affection. Support. All those finer instincts a husband is supposed to show, but which we nobles so seldom do."

"Well then!" Charles said, as he turned rather abruptly back toward the door to the hall. "Is there anything else you think I do not know about my betrothed?" he threw over his shoulder. It was not gently asked, and Godfrey could not fault him for being insulted.

Godfrey had no reply for a moment, and Charles was astonished to see The Blade lower those long, dark lashes over those usually piercing eyes, and to see the chin lower down to where it touched his chest. Charles had seen the man in lighter moods where he showed himself to be amused, frivolous, uncaring, lighthearted, and once or twice even softened, but he had never seen him this way before, at a loss, perhaps even humbled. It had always before been Charles who had turned away his eyes first, had tried to hide his thoughts, or emotions, or doubts beneath the weight of the man's knowing stare. The sight, so extraordinary, of The Blade allowing himself to be seen in less than complete command of himself was enough to soften the bite of Charles's next words. "And what if I were to tell you something of the lady, Rothayne? I will tell you, to ease your mind."

He turned away, now staring out the open doors as Godfrey had done before him, unsettled by that bowed head.

"I know that Mary is not passionately in love with me. Sometimes I think I see an affection . . . for someone else . . . and other times I think that is nothing more than just a reflection of Mary's sweet nature. I know . . . I like to think that we will deal well together. I also know full well that Mary is an innocent. Oh yes, she is clever, and quite aware of the ways of the world around her, yet for all of that, she is still an innocent. I have seen her looking upon me, judging me, yes, but too, it . . . it is as if she is searching me for . . . well, I do not know for what exactly. A kind of knowledge, I suppose. Marital knowledge, no doubt, I think. I see in her eyes that she is . . . struggling. And there is something else—something I betray only to you, for I know how close the two of you are—that though I have had the privilege of three kisses from the lady, they have been very chaste kisses, very circumspect."

Behind him, Godfrey slowly began to raise his head, a question flickering up into his eyes.

"Although I can only applaud her . . . er . . . *rectitude,* one could be excused for being surprised that a lady of her—well, face the truth!—a lady of her years is so . . . so well *sheltered,* let us say. One could be excused for expecting some more response than . . ." he gave a self- conscious laugh, "well, than your sister might give you."

The questioning light turned into a spark, as Godfrey stared unblinkingly at Charles' averted face.

"Don't get me wrong!" he said with some fervency, still staring out at nothing, choosing not to meet the steady stare. "I am pleased to find Mary of such fine, upstanding morality, and there's time enough for . . . refinements of behavior later! Still, one could hope for a *hint* of ardor, just a little flicker . . ." Charles frowned of a sudden, and then cleared his throat, frowning even more deeply as he fell into silent thought, obviously disturbed at something in the tenor of his own thoughts.

The silence hung between them, uncomfortable and awkward. Godfrey almost cried out, almost screamed at the fellow, horrified by his obliviousness. *Mary, passionless? Mary, filled with rectitude? Which Mary was this? It could not be Mary Wagnall!* Not the Mary who had kissed him back, had made him smile like a fool that he might not reach into her carriage and snatch her back into his

201

embrace! What kind of Mary did the man think he was to take to wife? Could Charles then so easily take and mold her into the very model of every other man's wife? Was that in fact what Charles really wanted, especially of Mary? And could *he*, Godfrey, bear it? To have Mary lose that which made her separate, different, special, wonderful? And to think he had helped her to achieve this point and place in time! Oh, it was a travesty, a misjustice, to each and every one of them. Yet, worst of all, by what right was he to say that such a life was not for her?

Finally Charles pushed back his shoulders, and lifted his chin. He said a trifle gruffly, "There is something specific I wished to ask of you, your grace. 'Tis why I came to search you out, for a moment alone together."

Godfrey waited, his eyes now straightly meeting those of Charles, only the faint drawing together of his brows reflecting his inner turmoil.

"I would ask of you a particular favor."

"Yes?" Godfrey said sharply. He leaned just as nonchalantly as ever against the doorframe, but his hands in his pockets were balled into tight fists.

"I would ask that you no longer refer to Mary as 'my pet', or 'my love', or 'my own'. You understand, I'm sure?"

Godfrey felt a bolt of lightning whip through his body, and for a moment he wondered if the fellow would also deny him food, water, breath, and life entirely, but with a great effort he managed a nod. "Of course," he croaked out.

"Do you leave our little party now, your grace?" Charles said, the broadest of all possible hints, and again Godfrey could not fault the man. It should, after all, be a day of only pleasure and gaiety for him.

Godfrey repeated, his voice barely a whisper, "Of course. Yes."

"Then I will meet you at the church tomorrow," Charles stated. "Please remember to bring the ring." He turned on his heel and made his exit, leaving the room filled with a darkness much deeper than the mere lack of light.

Godfrey sagged against the door jamb, the night breeze that caressed his face now feeling as cool as the hand of death against his overheated cheeks. "Mary!" he whispered into the night.

He did not know how long he stood there thusly, but in time he sensed that once again he was not alone. He lifted his head slowly, becoming aware that the observer must have been standing there a while, watching him as still and silently as he now observed her. It was a full minute until he again whispered the name, "Mary!"

She glided into the room, her eyes already adjusted to the darkness so that she bypassed the furnishings without difficulty. He stretched out his hands, and she slid hers into his as he came away from the doorframe at last. They stood, their hands joined between them, their eyes picking out the occasional luminescence of skin and eye that the moonglow afforded them.

"I thought perhaps you had left," she said, her voice low and quiet, but never scolding.

"I am about to."

"It has been a long evening. I think perhaps it was a mistake to make this party the night before the wedding." He heard the note of weariness in her voice.

"Yes," he said simply. "But you will be a beautiful, glowing bride come the morn, I know it."

"They say all brides are beautiful, but I think not I," she sighed. The darkness allowed her to be bold, letting her speak her thoughts aloud. Or perhaps it was more than just the darkness. For Godfrey had become her dearest friend, a truth brought home by the very warmth that had come back into her limbs the moment he had called her name and beckoned her into the circle of his presence. The party had been chilling and nearly unendurable, when it should have been all gaiety and merriment. And yet it had taken only these precious, stolen moments alone with him, which should have, by all rights, been an agony of separation and yet was filled with a quiet, pervading joy, to prove they indeed shared a sincere friendship.

"Mary, if you have never been told it, I tell you now: when all the 'pretties' have faded into frumpish old women, your fine face will still be graced by handsome lines and flattering color. Yours is to be the handsome grace of later life."

"Thank you," she whispered, clasping his hands even more tightly, for she knew he spoke only the truth. Tears came to her eyes, but they were not entirely unhappy tears.

"And now I have made you cry," he sighed, his hand coming away from hers to reach up and place a finger along the glistening trail that spilled over the lashes of one eye. With a kind of groan, he then pulled her gently into his arms, holding her to his chest and rocking slightly from side to side, as one might with a young child. "Ah, the dream at last, it is yours. Charles is a very lucky man."

"And soon you are to be lucky as well. Have you

offered for Miss Yardley yet?" Ah, the dark was a boon, that she might ask such a question, hidden from his clear eyes.

"I have not, nor shall I. She is a dear child, but nothing more to me. No, I'll not be walking the matrimonial path, not any time soon."

"Oh, Godfrey, I am so sorry—"

"Do not be. I am only glad to know it, even though it was not what I thought I wanted." He spoke to the top of her head, not letting her go, for they did not need to see one another's faces to communicate, not tonight.

He held her for a very long time, his eyes closing over the top of her head as realizations struck him as though they were blows. This was the last moment for such closeness. After tomorrow they could never again have the right to be so free with one another. For the sake of his friends, and their marriage, he would have to watch his tongue such as he had never done with her before. He could never again hold her with such unmeasured physical closeness, for Charles would be the ever-present shield between them. He would never again feel the warmth of her breath as it skittered across his neck and his ear, never find himself in such a close and silent embrace that he could feel and hear her heartbeat as though it were his own. And—most frightening and overwhelming of all—he doubted he would ever again hold a woman who meant so much to him that the ache in his soul far outstretched the aching of his body for her. A physical passion was there, a kind of quiet peeping he heard beneath the roar of the anguish and longing for her, her essence, her deepest being, that filled his brain, so that he began to wonder if he could ever be strong enough to open his arms and let her walk out of them.

A voice was heard, calling from down the hall, first his name and then hers.

"Hortense!" Godfrey identified the voice with some astonishment, like a man waking from a dream.

Mary turned up her face in the darkness, her arms staying as they were, not moving to disentangle themselves from him. Instead, the sound of the searcher coming nearer seemed to stir her. "Will you not be the first to kiss the bride?" she asked in the merest whisper. For a kiss must be the end of this sweet embrace, she knew, and the end of her foolish dreams.

He could not resist such an invitation, nor did he try. His mouth came down on hers, and there was only openness and responsiveness, and an eagerness to touch his mouth in return with hers. Her hands went at once to the nape of his neck, as though to hold him there with her forever, as though to say that she, too, could not bear to end what they both knew was in truth a kind of final parting. She pressed into him, allowing him to know even more that the kiss was not given as to a friend, but as to a lover. Just as he thought to pull away, to say something, to try to comprehend what was happening, she gave a pain-filled sob and was gone from him, flown from the room before he could even put out a hand to stop her.

He stood, a trembling coming over him so that his teeth actually chattered, and his breath was taken only in ragged gulps. He turned to the doorframe once more, his shaking hands reaching to hold the solid wood, that his strengthless legs might not give out beneath him. He pressed his forehead to the unbending wood, closed his eyes and willed some bit of sanity to return to his fevered brain.

And then he found himself chortling, then laughing mirthlessly, for Mary had betrayed Charles with that kiss, that passionate kiss. His Mary, the one whom he had known to be better than all others, had betrayed the man she was to marry. It could only make him think of Melinda and Sandra. Only this time, it was *he* who helped her to the betrayal, and it was Charles who must play the part of cuckold. But the strangest thing of all: he could not care. The laughter died on his lips in realization. He could not be disappointed by her disloyalty, for she was nothing at all like the others. Melinda and Sandra had been trying to better their positions in life by what they did, whereas Mary was . . . Mary was . . . what? Why were the kisses she gave Charles, as the man had claimed, "chaste and circumspect", and yet this one she had given him all that could blister a man inside and out with its radiance? Was Mary, then, actually capable of such deceit and cunning that she was making an attempt to persuade him that his stand against marriage must not include herself? No, no, a thousand times no, he would swear it. Hadn't he held the truth in his arms tonight? They had had that moment of such closeness; he would have known had she been lying to him, or pretending. No, that was not the way of his Mary.

He sighed deeply and shivered in the garden breeze, too overwhelmed by the thought that Mary had merely, and simply, wanted his kiss, to be able to move.

Mary was discovered by Hortense in a moment's time. That lady looked at Mary's flushed face, and inquired, "Are you all right, Mary?"

"Fine. Quite fine," Mary said with eyes that were too bright. "I took some air, and now I am quite fine."

She let Hortense lead her back to the party. She found herself laughing, laughing at the smallest thing, for she could not keep the near hysteria that filled her lungs from escaping, and better it be done in laughter than in screams. And, too, the rather wild-eyed amusement she showed might account for the flighty, trembling nature of her hands, and the way her whole body shook from time to time.

Hortense saw the overly bright eyes, the giddy attitude, and frowned at it. It was unnatural, a little crazed. She looked up then and caught the eye of the companion, of Mrs. Pennett. That face was grave, saddened, filled with despair for her dear charge.

Suddenly Hortense knew that Mary had not been alone in the back room of the house. She knew it for a certainty. Abruptly she left Mary's side, but the bride-to-be was too far lost to the effort of forced gaiety to notice.

"Godfrey," a hushed voice penetrated his frozen solitude, but he did not move, half hoping she would not know he was there. He was out of luck, though, for Hortense came into the room. "You're here?" she asked, but just as soon as she asked, she spotted him, and crossed to his side. "Why, Godfrey, you are shaking!" she cried as her hand touched his arm. "Let me close these doors—"

"No, leave them. It . . . it is not the breeze which chills me."

"What then?" she asked, anxiety creeping into her voice.

"I . . . it is this wedding. I am not sure Mary should marry Charles. I am not sure they are suited."

"Well, why not?" She tried to pull him toward the inner room, hoping to take a chair, to light a lamp, but he would not come with her.

"She . . . I . . . I kissed her now, and, well, it was not the way . . . it just seems to me that a woman ought not to betray a man the night before she marries him." Of course, he did not believe a word of it, but at least it was an explanation to give Hortense.

"Oh, Godfrey, when will you ever let us women get down off our pedestals?" she cried in exasperation. "Mary is one of the finest creatures I have ever met. That she kissed you, well, what of it? We women are just as you men—able to make mistakes, and to correct them, too. She's excited. She's overwrought. And she's also imperfect. Yes, just like the rest of us."

He just shook his head.

"Godfrey," Hortense cried, understanding having come as soon as she had looked into his and Mary's faces. "That's not what's important. You know what is: why are you letting her marry Charles? You love her, don't you?"

He put his hands to his face, shuddered, and did not answer.

"Why don't you ask her to marry *you?* I'll tell you why," she cried when still he could not answer. "You'll never take a wife. You'll never be happy, because you'll never find the perfect woman."

"You're wrong," he said gruffly, his hands dropping as he turned to her with a sharp gesture. "I've never wanted a perfect woman."

She grabbed both his arms, so that his shadowed face was near hers. "The truth now, brother. You want a good woman, and yet one that can enjoy your wicked wit. You've found that in Mary, and only Mary. What is truly disturbing you is that it is Bretwyn who shall have her, and not yourself. You silly, stupid fool! Why can you not just ask her if she'll have you instead of him?"

"I am not good enough for her. No, Hortense, you know it as well as I. Do not deny it. I've bedded dozens of women. I've never been faithful to any of them. I've failed miserably in my sad attempts to bring any woman to wife. I've been banished from the realm—"

"No more."

"—and I've played games, always games with her."

"On terms she accepted. She's no fool. Why do you treat her like one?" Hortense cried, for it was clear to see that Godfrey was in misery. Why had she not seen it before? When he had lightly called the woman 'his Mary' it had not been in fun, as even he had thought, for his heart had taken him seriously.

"It's too late. She deserves Bretwyn. He'll bring her stability—"

"So could you."

"Could I? I have no record of such fidelity," he said bitterly.

"Don't let your past ruin your future."

"Hortense, leave me. Please, as you love me, leave me. I cannot think. I—I just need to be alone."

She drew back, slowly nodding her head. Yes, let their words penetrate that stubborn brain. Perhaps . . . maybe . . . there was a chance he might hear what had been said.

She left him, without another word, though she kissed his cheek before she left.

In a little while Godfrey went out through the

double doors into the gardens, closing the doors behind himself with the care and deliberateness of a man too agitated to do anything but what he ought, and made his way blindly to his carriage. His ostler was startled out of a light doze, the horses were quickly rigged to the vehicle, and Godfrey was borne gratefully and quietly away from the party which was to honor two of the few he had come to admire in this world.

Chapter Eighteen

Morning brought with it a ceasing to the shivers that had possessed him in the night, but, too, it brought an unexpected visitor. "Godfrey!" Hortense had cried stridently, opening his door to his chambers without so much as a knock, and despite the frantic efforts of his valet to steer her away.

"What do you want?" he growled from his bed, the bed wherein he had done very little sleeping as he tossed through the night.

"I let you sleep all night on it, and now I want to talk to you about this whole silly marriage business." She reached for the robe his wide-eyed valet was holding at the ready, and tossed it her brother's way. It landed on his head, spilling down over his face.

From beneath the material she heard him say, "Go away, you gorgon."

"Get up at once," was her immediate response.

He pulled the robe from his head, sighing, for the past had taught him that Hortense would not be dissuaded by so little a thing as someone else's wishes.

"Let me dress. You can talk at me in the carriage. In case you've forgotten, I must be a best man this morning," he said hollowly.

Across town, Mary looked around the small room wonderingly. It was not that she did not recall how she had come to be there, it was rather that she could not believe she had been able to do so. She had forced herself to operate on two levels. On the one she went about the business of getting dressed in the taffeta wedding gown and veil. She made sure the flowers were as they ought to be. She saw to all of the tiny details that her mother, sister, father, brother, not to mention any number of aunts, uncles and cousins thought to throw her way. Yet, on the other side of her mind, she was in the middle of a battlefield. That side of her was warning her to flee, to desist, to change her mind, to deny the day, to cease the plans.

She heard her own internal arguments, and did her best to ignore them.

It's time to marry.

How can I marry him?

This was exactly what you were expecting! Why cavil now?

But Charles doesn't deserve this . . . doesn't deserve this lack of affection!

Don't be foolish!

I'm not whole. He doesn't deserve half a person.

And what would make you whole?

There was only one answer to that, and she dare not even let herself think it.

Her mother looked over and saw that her daughter's eyes were once again beginning to roll back into her head. "Hartshorn!" she cried.

Lydia pressed the vial into her mother's hand, which was waved again under Mary's nose. Her nose wrinkled, her eyes slid back into place, and she thrust out a hand to push the vile smell away. "I'm all right!" she gasped.

"You are *not* all right," her mother chided. "That's the third time this morning. Are you ill?" She put her mouth near her daughter's ear and whispered urgently, "You aren't expecting, are you?"

"Of course not!" Mary cried, blushing and feeling a little faint again when she did. "I'm just nervous."

"Well, I never saw such a case of nerves."

The door opened and Charles stood there, an anxious look on his face. He seemed on the verge of saying something, but at the last minute switched and said instead, "Everyone ready? The music is just about to begin."

"Charles Bretwyn! Get out at once!" Lady Cornelia cried, coming at him while making shooing motions. "You're not supposed to see the bride before the wedding."

"It *is* the wedding," he said matter-of-factly.

"Go on now."

The door was shut, but not before Mary had a glimpse of the best man, Godfrey, standing silently a few steps behind Charles. For a moment their eyes had met, but then the door had been closed between them. She had seen Hortense there, too, at her brother's side, speaking rapidly near his ear.

"Men!" her mother scolded, coming back to take her daughter's elbow and help her to her feet.

Mary tottered for a moment, but the sudden dizziness was fleeting. She tried to give her mother a small smile, but she did not doubt it must have more closely resembled a grimace.

Then there was the music, and her mother was led away on the arm of Randolph, and it was her father's arm to which she now clung. He led her from the little room, and she stood at the back of the church with him. She looked away from where Mrs. Pennett stood in the last row of the church, a kerchief pressed to her mouth, her dear eyes filled with a regret that Mary could not bear to look upon. Hortense was at Mrs. Pennett's side, frowning furiously. Mary looked up the aisle, saw Charles and Godfrey exchanging low, soft words, and saw Charles put his hand to his chin, his brow first puckered, then smoothed. He may even have nodded faintly.

Godfrey turned and strode down the aisle, and Mary felt a new trembling coming over her. She closed her eyes, half wishing him already gone from the church, that she might not have to look upon him this sad day. But she knew he had stopped before her, and she forced her eyes open.

He had a slightly sheepish look on his face, and he seemed to be struggling for words.

"We've a wedding to hold," her father said, frowning with disapproval at the duke.

"Do you love Charles?" Godfrey asked Mary, his blue eyes never having left her face.

She shook her head, and said in a very small voice, "No."

Lord Wagnall's eyes rounded in his head, and he cried as he glared at the Duke, " 'Tis only wedding day nerves speaking!"

"I am all wrong for you, Mary. I am the worst of souls, and you are the finest. Hortense has been buzzing in my ear all morning, and yet all I could think was that you deserve a better man than me. You deserve Charles," Godfrey said somberly. He then said, "Excuse me," finally bothering to give Lord Wagnall a flicker of a glance. He reached out both hands, physically removed Mary's hand from where it lay on her father's arm, and turned and walked forward, back down the aisle toward Charles, her hand now planted on his arm. Lord Wagnall glared at their backs, and raised his hands to tousle his hair in agitation, unable to decide if he should make even more a spectacle of the whole affair by dashing after them and demanding that the duke leave at once. He looked to his wife, who only confused him more when she pointed and shook her head, gestures whose meaning he could not decipher.

"Godfrey," Mary cried, tears in her voice as well as her eyes. She had been able to force herself this far, to lie to herself, until he touched her. "I can't. I can't possibly."

"It's too late," Godfrey said simply.

He stopped before the vicar, standing next to Mary, Charles on her other side. Her hand dropped lifelessly, his own hands coming together in a light clasp before him. "Get on with it," he ordered the vicar.

Charles leaned forward to glance at him around Mary, but then he turned back to the vicar, who had begun the ceremony. The vicar spoke for several moments, instructing the assembly as to why they were all gathered this day, and then he moved on to the vows.

"Do you, Charles Anthony Bretwyn, take this—"

"Not *him!*" Godfrey interrupted.

"Not *me!*" Charles said at the same time.

"*I'm* the one she's marrying," Godfrey went on, as Charles nodded complacently at Mary's side.

Four hundred gasps filled the room, one of which belonged to no less a person than Mary herself.

"But . . . but you said it was too late!" Mary

cried, flashing a completely puzzled glance at Charles that took in his benign expression, only to turn and cast her question up at Godfrey in confusion.

Godfrey turned to her, plainly astonished. "I meant it was too late for you to get out of being stuck with me. I know I am the worst of fellows, which I prove again by insisting you must marry me anyway, but it is too bad. You *must* have me."

"Oh, Godfrey . . ." she whispered, sudden joy filling her so that she began to tremble. Tears of happiness filled her eyes, rolling unheeded down her cheeks. "Can you really mean it?"

"Of course I mean it."

"What is this? Father Trundell, I must insist that you desist!" Lord Wagnall cried as he came storming forward.

"Oh, nonsense. Let's just get on with the thing," Charles said calmly. "I *thought* I saw a *tendre* had formed between you two," he said down to Mary with a slightly rueful smile. "When Godfrey there informed me that he would have to kill either me or himself before he could let me wed 'his Mary', well, then, there was nothing for it but to gracefully step back. Truth be told, I'm not quite sure I was prepared to say 'yes' myself. I hope you can forgive my hesitation, and I rather suppose I might have asked how you felt about the thing, but I am afraid your face has quite given you away."

There was a flurry of gasps and hand clappings from the back of the church, and a quick glance showed that Hortense and Mrs. Pennett were hugging one another when they were not applauding.

"Unfortunately, I'm afraid that although I offer you my complete felicitations, I must point out that

217

you do not have a marriage license for today's change in events."

Her father interjected, "Mary! Never say you want to marry this Rothayne fellow, this rake, this . . . cad!"

"I do. I want it with my whole heart," she said. "Oh, Papa, I really thought I should marry Charles." She turned to Charles again, contrition marking her features. "Charles, I'm so sorry!"

"No, no. Love triumphs, and all that," he said, smiling at her in a way that told her whatever pangs he felt now would soon be forgotten, if it meant she was to marry where her heart lay. She did not even try to stop herself, throwing herself into his arms and hugging him tightly even as she planted a kiss on his cheek. He blushed a little, and then laughed a little, then took her hands from his shoulders and placed them in Godfrey's.

"But he's right, Mary," Godfrey said to her. "I have no license hiding in my pocket. I came here, planning to be the good fellow and see you safely wedded to a fine, upstanding man. Hortense told me what a fool I was, and in my heart I knew it was true, but all the same I was going to be good to you, you see, but I have failed. Failed entirely. You find yourself in the middle of a terrible scandal, which is all my doing."

"Godfrey, you goose. It's not all your doing, for am I not the one saying I want you? *You* are my fine, upstanding man."

"I am not. I am 'The Blade', a man of outrageous reputation."

"It is that very reputation that will carry us through. Yes, some of the sticklers will never forgive us this day, but how can I care for that? All I care about is that you love me."

He grew deadly serious. "I'll never play you false," he said.

"You see? Oh, Godfrey. But I must hear you say it, for you will never say what you do not mean."

He smiled then, for she knew him so well. There were four hundred witnesses present to hear whatever The Blade might have to say. "Mary, I could not let you marry Charles, for, quite simply, I love you myself."

Another gasp went through the crowd, followed by yet another as Mary was caught up in the Duke's arms and roundly kissed. Mrs. Pennett gave a squeal of delight, fanning her face with a kerchief while Hortense jumped up and down in one spot.

"Your grace!" the vicar cried, looking from noble face to face, unsure how to proceed.

"Oh, go ahead and marry us, good Father," Godfrey said as he pulled his lips from Mary's, though he did not take his arms from her. "Even though it will be only for show today. Then we'll get our special license and be truly married three days hence. But why spoil the party now?"

"Your grace, I do not think—" the vicar began a protest.

"Oh, get on with it, man!" Lord Wagnall cried, his face brightly colored, though whether from vexation or relief, no man could say for sure. He mumbled on, "Told the wife that Mary wasn't acting as a bride ought. Fainting all over the place, and all. At least now I understand it . . ."

The vicar cleared his throat, then announced, "Er . . . it seems that . . . things have changed. I cannot perform a marriage ceremony, as the . . . er . . . consenting couple do not have a license, but I will . . . I will . . ." he hit on sudden inspiration, "I will give them a Ceremony of Blessing! Would everyone please be seated?"

"Lady Wagnall," Godfrey said in a low voice even as he turned in preparation to receive the vicar's blessing, "I will warn you now, before we proceed any further, that you simply do not have the option of discontinuing *this* betrothal. Not after all these observers have witnessed my protestations of love."

"No, I do not," she smiled.

"You do, however, have the option of beginning the honeymoon tonight," he added in the familiar, beloved, teasing way he had.

"No, I do not," she laughed, but there was real regret in her voice even as she said it.

"Three days, and then I shall not accept that response," he said throatily.

"Three days," she sighed as the vicar began to speak.

And so, though they exchanged no earthly vows this day, and had no rings to make a public binding, and were sure to be unwelcome past certain doors due to their public and vulgar display of affection and devotion, Mary left the church on Godfrey's arm in complete contentment. The three days flew past, and they ventured forth to Kent, where a true and binding wedding ceremony took place amidst dozens of relatives. The previously missing brothers-in-law met Mary for the first time, and Mary's siblings and extended family members were there as well. Her siblings gave the newlywed a special gift: a set of atrociously gaudy house slippers, which had occasioned much laughter. Many other, and more lovely gifts, of course, were forthcoming from the many females of Godfrey's family.

The celebrational parties lasted three days, at which time Godfrey took his bride in exasperation onto a ship to sail to southern climes, far removed from anyone they knew.

Thirteen months later he sat amidst his family. It could at last be said that he had truly become the master of his home, which was, it must further be said, due in large part to the fact that his family was so delighted with his choice of bride. They actually came to respect the newlyweds' need for privacy, and left them to themselves at Rothayne Manor, except for holidays, of course. On this day, thirteen months and ten days after the wedding, they had gathered yet again in those halls. It was a measure of their awareness of the master's upset that they walked and spoke quietly, pausing occasionally to pat him on the shoulder or offer him a sip of tea or brandy. He sat staring out an open door, toward the closed door at the opposite end of the long corridor.

At last the other door opened, and he rose swiftly to his feet, moving forward until he was nearly running. It was his mother come to bring him the news.

"She's fine," his mother said.

"Thank God," he breathed, then he added, "And was it twins?"

"It was." She had no more time to add more, for he swept past her.

He threw open the door, belatedly remembering that it might be better to slow his progress, and saw his wife lying in their bed, which several of his sisters were putting to rights around her.

"Oh, Godfrey!" Hortense scolded. "We were scarce ready for you yet."

"Mary," he said, ignoring his sister, and moving to step around the bed to her side. There were the two

221

little forms on either side of her, so bundled as to be indistinguishable from the bedding if it were not for the tiny squawks that each was emitting. "You are all right?" He leaned over her, planting a relieved kiss on her forehead, for although she was pale and looked wearied as he'd never seen her, he did see the dancing light in her eyes that told him everything was fine.

"Yes. I'm very tired, but I'm all right."

He saw then that the dancing light in those beloved eyes was caused by a deep amusement. "Godfrey," she said, a laugh — weak but still filled with mirth — coming with the words, "I don't know how to tell you this. We have twin *daughters*."

He looked down at her, kissed her again, and said, "Thank you so much. I really mean it, really," so that she knew he did. He reached out his arms to be given a child to hold as she held the other, and could only join her and everyone else in the room in happily exasperated laughter.

ZEBRA'S HOLIDAY REGENCY ROMANCES CAPTURE THE MAGIC OF EVERY SEASON

THE VALENTINE'S DAY BALL (3280, $3.95)
by Donna Bell

Tradition held that at the age of eighteen, all the Heartland ladies met the man they would marry at the Valentine's Day Ball. When she was that age, the crucial ball had been canceled when Miss Jane Lindsey's mother had died. Now Jane was on the shelf at twenty-four. Still, she was happy in her life and accepted the fact that romance had passed her by. So she was annoyed with herself when the scandalous—and dangerously handsome—Lord Devlin put a schoolgirl blush into her cheeks and made her believe that perhaps romance may *indeed* be a part of her life . . .

AN EASTER BOUQUET (3330, $3.95)
by Therese Alderton

It was a preposterous and scandalous wager: In return for a prime piece of horse-flesh, the decadent Lord Vyse would pose as a virtuous Rector in a country village. His cohorts insisted he wouldn't last a week, yet he was actually looking forward to a quiet Easter in the country.

Miss Lily Sterling was puzzled by the new rector; he had a reluctance to discuss his past and looked at her the way no Rector should *ever* look at a female of his flock. She was determined to unmask this handsome "clergyman", and she would set herself up as his bait!

A CHRISTMAS AFFAIR (3244, $3.95)
by Joan Overfield

Justin Stockman thought he was doing the Laurence family a favor by marrying the docile sister and helping the family reverse their financial straits. The first thing he would do after the marriage was to marry off his independent and infuriating sister-in-law Amanda.

Amanda was intent on setting the arrogant Justin straight on a few matters, and the cozy holiday backdrop—from the intimate dinners to the spectacular Frost Fair—would be the perfect opportunities to let him know what life would be like with her as a sister-in-law. She would give a Merry Christmas indeed!

A CHRISTMAS HOLIDAY (3245, $3.95)

A charming collection of Christmas short stories by Zebra's best Regency Romance writers. *The Holly Brooch, The Christmas Bride, The Glastonbury Thorn, The Yule Log, A Mistletoe Christmas,* and *Sheer Sorcery* will give you the warmth of the Holiday Season all year long.